"This Isn't A Joke, Michael.

"I take my work very seriously. But then, you're the man who could never take *anything* seriously."

Michael reached across the desk and caught her hand. It was stiff under his, and he squeezed. "Some things never change, do they?"

Unnerved, Katherine slid her hand from his. "How did you hear about the experiment?"

He shrugged. "At the bar. Some of your students were talking about it."

She glanced down at her hands and realized in dismay that she was rhythmically stroking the place where Michael's had covered hers. She dropped them to her lap.

"They said you were too old."

"What!"

"Too old," he repeated blandly.

"I heard you the first time," she muttered. When she got her hands on them she would—

"So tell me, Katie..." He leaned toward her and lowered his voice to a conspiratorial whisper. "What are you too old for?"

Dear Reader:

Happy Holidays from all of us at Silhouette Books. And since it *is* the holiday season, we've planned an extra special month at Silhouette Desire. Think of it as our present to you, the readers.

To start with, we have December's *Man of the Month*, who comes in the tantalizing form of Tad Jackson in Ann Major's *Wilderness Child*. This book ties into the Children of Destiny series, but Tad's story also stands on its own. Believe me, Tad's a man you'd *love* to find under your Christmas tree.

And what would December be without a Christmas book? We have a terrific one—*Christmas Stranger* by Joan Hohl. After you've read it, I'm sure you'll understand why I say this is a truly timeless love story.

Next, don't miss book one of Celeste Hamilton's trilogy, Aunt Eugenia's Treasures. *The Diamond's Sparkle* is just the first of three priceless love stories. Look for *Ruby Fire* and *Hidden Pearl* in February and April of 1990.

Finally, some wonderful news: the *Man of the Month* will be continued through 1990! We just couldn't resist bringing you one more year of these stunning men. In the upcoming months you'll be seeing brand-new *Man of the Month* books by Elizabeth Lowell, Annette Broadrick and Diana Palmer—just to name a few. Barbara Boswell will make her Silhouette Desire debut with her man. I'll be keeping you updated....

Before I go, I want to wish all of our readers a very Happy Holiday. See you next year!

Lucia Macro
Senior Editor

ERICA SPINDLER

READ BETWEEN THE LINES

SILHOUETTE *Desire*

Published by Silhouette Books New York

America's Publisher of Contemporary Romance

SILHOUETTE BOOKS
300 East 42nd St., New York, N.Y. 10017

ERICA SPINDLER

came to writing from the visual arts and has numerous one-person, invitational and group exhibitions to her credit. She still teaches art classes in addition to her writing. "It seems only natural to me that I should be writing romance," says Erica. "My paintings had the same spirit of optimism and romanticism that my stories do."

A descendant of Marie Duplessis, who was the most famous courtesan of her day and the inspiration for Dumas's work *Camille*, Erica lives with her husband in New Orleans, where she does most of her writing in a penthouse that affords a panoramic view of that intriguing, history-rich city.

For my friends
Without you, life wouldn't be nearly so bright
Thank you

One

—

Excuse me?'' Katherine Reed leveled her frostiest stare at the man sitting across from her.

He shifted uncomfortably. ''Nothing. Forget it.''

''Yes, I think we'd better.'' Katherine's gaze swept over him. She disliked the petulant tilt of his lips even more than the skintight leather pants he was wearing. ''That concludes your interview, Mr. Anderson. If you've been chosen for the experiment, you'll hear from us within the week.''

Over my dead body, Katherine silently added, watching him walk away. She still couldn't believe he'd had the nerve to ask her what she wore to bed! As if sex was part of the deal! What a scumbucket.

Who would think a nice, conservative town like Rockford, Illinois, would have so many weirdos? she wondered, untying the silk scarf at her neck and dropping it to the desk. And more, who would have suspected they would all show up to apply for a college sociology experiment?

With a small sigh, she massaged the tense muscles at the nape of her neck. Every spring, her first-year graduate students were required to propose, participate in and document a sociological study. Traditionally, as a sign that she considered them professionals whose theories were worthy of her respect, she also participated. Until now, that hadn't been a problem. Last year's group had studied the social interaction and behavior transformation that take place in women's organizations. The project had been interesting, the results enlightening.

But this year's students—she sighed again—had come up with something more challenging and much more provocative. They wanted to study the effect of cohabitation on behavior. And there was only one way to proceed—actual cohabitation.

She'd always considered herself lucky to have landed a teaching position at a school as progressive as this one. For a small, private institution, Rock River College had an excellent reputation in the scientific community, and they spared no expense in maintaining that reputation.

Katherine looked down at the stack of questionnaires and resisted the urge to sigh again. At this moment she didn't feel lucky. Finding a partner for herself was proving even more difficult than she'd expected. The man before Leather Legs had asked if there would be room for his fourteen cats, three dogs and pet raccoon. Earlier that evening, she'd interviewed a religious fanatic—she still wasn't sure what religion—and a man who'd reeked of gin. The only thing missing tonight had been nice, normal, average.

Katherine rolled her shoulders in an attempt to loosen the muscles, then took a deep breath. They couldn't get any worse than the last two. It wasn't possible. Not really believing her own assurances, she stood to call out the next number.

Then she saw him—Michael Tardo, proverbial bad boy from her past. He was talking to Marilyn and Ron Fuss, the students heading up the experiment. Her heart leaped to her throat. What was Michael doing here?

Knowing she should either call out the next number or sit down, Katherine stared at him, her mouth dry, her palms damp. He hadn't changed since their years together at Northern Illinois University—he was still broad-shouldered and lean; his dark, curly hair as thick and unruly as it had ever been. And he still dressed with casual panache. Black jeans faded to a rich charcoal outlined all the right places; the sleeves of his red sweater were pushed up, revealing muscular forearms.

Katherine realized she was staring at the place where fabric met flesh, and tore her eyes away. Pulling herself up to her full five feet one inch, she squared her shoulders and sternly reminded herself she was immune to Michael Tardo's macho brand of good looks.

Katherine drew her eyebrows together in thought. Shortly after her arrival in Rockford she'd learned Michael owned a popular college bar in the city. That hadn't surprised her—she knew he had family here. But she was surprised to see him now, in this place. Academia was hardly his kind of scene, nor was a group of intellectuals his usual choice of companions. He was probably dating one of the coeds, she thought. A blonde, no doubt. One with a great figure and—

Just then Michael turned his head and their eyes met. In one heart-stopping flash, Katherine remembered everything about him, from the way he smelled after a workout to the way he'd looked racing across campus on his motorcycle. And in that moment it seemed as if the eight years they'd been apart had slipped away and they were once again the best of friends, sharing jokes and dreams, laughter and disappointment.

Michael lifted his hand in a playful salute and smiled. The curving of his lips was slow, easy and unabashedly sexy, and Katherine's pulse fluttered. Swearing softly, she looked away.

After eight years she was still acting the fool over Michael Tardo. The truth of that grated on her nerves, and she called number twenty-two, then sat back down. She furiously tapped the stack of forms in front of her into a neat pile. Why couldn't she have stood, called her number and not seen him? Sometimes life wasn't fair— first, men wearing leather, now, Michael. Could this night get any worse?

"What do you think?" Michael Tardo asked, cocking his head as he considered the harried young woman in front of him.

Marilyn Fuss slipped off her glasses and nervously rubbed the lenses with the edge of her jacket. "I don't know. It seems like a perfect solution."

"Exactly what I thought." Michael smiled reassuringly. Solutions were why he was here. To Katherine's problems—and his own.

"In fact," Marilyn said, sounding suddenly more confident, "I imagine Dr. Reed will be relieved."

Michael followed the woman's glance. A moment ago Katherine had been interviewing a man who'd dressed as if he owned stock in a leather company. The man sitting across from her now was gesturing wildly as he spoke. She looked frustrated. "I see what you mean," he muttered.

"Believe me, you haven't seen anything." Marilyn's voice lowered to a whisper when Michael's eyes met hers again. "The bottom of the barrel."

"So I heard," Michael murmured, remembering what Katherine's students had told him a couple of nights ago at the bar. That's when he'd gotten the idea he might be able to kill two birds with one stone. Michael glanced back at Katherine. Her applicant was gone and she was staring pensively into space as she rubbed the back of her neck. She was an interesting woman; he'd thought so from the first. She was intelligent, outspoken and giving—all to a fault.

And lovely. Even back at school, with her Coke-bottle lenses and boxy, banged haircut, he'd thought so. Tonight her hair was pulled away from her face in a simple, if severe, style but it was still the color of midnight. Her thick lashes and fine brows were just as dark and framed the same startling blue eyes. Those eyes, he knew from experience, could flash like gemstones in the sun or be as icy as a frozen lake.

Other than her coloring, everything about Katherine was delicate, from her tiny but perfectly proportioned body to her flawless porcelain skin and finely chiseled features. But Michael knew her too well to be fooled by appearances; Katherine had a backbone of steel, iron-clad determination and a sharp wit.

She stood up to call her next number and looked at him. He saw the question in her eyes and felt the oddest pang. There had been a time when she would have expected to see him, a time when they spent more hours together than apart. What had happened to their friendship?

Just as he started to smile, Marilyn tapped him on the elbow.

"You know, Michael, my husband and...oh, Dr. Reed's called your number." Marilyn tucked her clipboard under her arm. "Good luck."

"Thanks," Michael murmured, then crossed to Katherine. She'd returned to her seat and didn't look up as he approached. He stopped in front of the desk. "Hello, Katie."

Katherine gritted her teeth at the annoying nickname at the same moment her heart flip-flopped. Ignoring both, she lifted her eyes. "Hello, Michael." Her voice sounded unusually husky, and she cleared her throat.

He leaned against the desk. "How's it going?"

He flashed her another of his breath-stealing smiles, and she busied herself with the already straightened stack of papers. "Fine...just fine. How are you?"

"Good." His eyes slid over her. "You look great."

"Oh..." It was all she could do to keep from squirming in her seat. She forced an indifferent smile. "Thanks."

He picked up her subtly toned scarf and ran it idly through his fingers. The delicate fabric felt unbelievably good against his skin. "Pretty."

Katherine watched as the silk slithered back and forth through his fingers. With a rush of heat, she realized what she was doing and jerked her gaze away. "Michael, I'm in the middle of interviewing...is there something you wanted?"

"Yeah." He slid his questionnaire on top of the stack in front of her. "Number twenty-three."

Katherine lowered her eyes. The form was filled in with the bold scrawl she remembered from years ago. A strange trembling started in the pit of her stomach, then moved upward. She and Michael living together? Even under the auspices of science it was ludicrous. She sucked in a deep, steadying breath. "You can't be serious."

She wasn't surprised now, she was stunned. Michael liked her reaction and grinned. "But I am."

"This is a scientific experiment, Michael. Not one of your fraternity games."

"You're studying the effect of cohabitation on behavior." He saw her eyes heat and his smile deepened. "You know me—could I pass up something as provocative as cohabitation?"

Even though only minutes before she'd used the same adjective to describe the study, it rankled coming from Michael. She counted to three before she spoke. When she did, her voice was tightly controlled. "This isn't a joke, Michael. I take my work very seriously. But then, you're the man who could never take *anything* seriously."

Michael reached across the desk and caught her hand. It was stiff under his, and he squeezed. "Some things never change, do they?"

Unnerved, Katherine slid her hand from his. "How did you hear about the experiment?"

He shrugged. "At the bar. Some of your students were talking about it. They seemed pretty tickled with themselves."

She glanced down at her hands and realized in dismay that she was rhythmically stroking the place where Michael's had covered hers. She dropped them to her lap. "How much did they tell you?"

He sank into the chair across from her. "After about a dozen beers, they told me quite a lot."

Great, she thought. So much for the social scientist's shy, egghead image.

Michael laughed and met her eyes. "After discussing interaction relations and causal points of view—"

"Interactionist perspectives and causal relationships," she corrected automatically.

"Right." Unperturbed, Michael relaxed against the chair back. "After that, they said you were too old."

"What!"

"Too old," he repeated blandly.

"I heard you the first time," she muttered. When she got her hands on them she would—

"So tell me, Katie—" he leaned toward her and lowered his voice to a conspiratorial whisper "—what are you too old for?"

His eyes were alight with humor and the blood rushed to her cheeks. "Nothing! The groups are going to consist of people who are close in age, that's all. Finding a partner for me is more difficult because the college-age applicants won't..." Her voice trailed off as she saw he was laughing at her. She stiffened. "Why are you doing this, Michael? You certainly don't need a place to live, or the two hundred bucks we pay."

"No. "But *you* need *me*."

For a moment she felt as giddy as a schoolgirl, then reality set in. He was doing the same thing he'd done in college—appointing himself her protector, her guardian. The last thing she needed was a big brother. "You're mistaken. I said finding a partner would be difficult, not impossible."

"My motives are far from selfless. Being your partner in the experiment would help me, too."

Katherine cocked her head and arched her brows in disbelief. "How so?" she asked, her tone grudging.

He stared at a point over her left shoulder for a moment, then looked back at her. He wasn't sure why, but he suddenly wished he didn't have to tell her about Susi Steele. "This is going to sound silly, but here goes. An old friend of mine has a daughter who's suddenly developed a crush on me. It's crazy, since I've known her since she was about ten. Well, now she's twenty and..." He cleared his throat. "I thought it would blow over, but it hasn't. She's really pursuing me and—"

Always a woman, Katherine thought nastily. She should have known. "And you don't want to hurt her."

"Yes," he said softly. "She's fragile...and I don't want anything to interfere with my friendship with her father."

"You think she'll bow out gracefully if you're living with someone else?"

"Nobody would get hurt."

Nobody but herself. "Sorry, Michael, it wouldn't work."

Something he'd thought just a good option before, now seemed urgent. He tipped his hands palms up. "Why not? What better choice do you have? Mr. Leather Pants?"

She lifted her chin. "For one thing, this is a scientific study. There are variables to be considered, variables that could eliminate you."

Michael bit back a smile. Talking to Marilyn beforehand was about to pay off. "Oh? I can't imagine what. I've never been married, or lived with a member of the opposite sex. Nor have we ever been romantically involved."

Katherine blanched at the last. No, as far as he remembered they'd never been romantically involved. She curled her fingers into her palms. "You can say that again."

"See? We're the perfect couple."

She'd thought so, too, a long time ago. Katherine hoped he wouldn't hear the hint of desperation in her voice as she said, "But we're old friends. I'm sure Marilyn and Ron would disqualify you on the basis of our past relationship."

"I already checked." Michael settled back in the chair and folded his arms across his chest. "Marilyn said there wouldn't be a problem."

Live with Michael? The thought made her light-headed. "This is crazy; this makes no sense."

"It makes perfect sense." He leaned toward her once again. "It solves both our problems. I avoid hurting a friend's daughter; you get out of living with someone who fills their closet with leather."

Katherine brought her hand to the back of her neck again. "I'm not sure—"

"What's not to be sure about?" he pressed. "We're old friends; living together should be a breeze. Why are you so opposed to this?"

Katherine dropped her hands to her lap. What could she say? That she was opposed because years ago she'd loved him and she wasn't certain she could remain immune to him if they lived together? Or because they'd shared a night of passion he didn't even remember?

"Katherine," he coaxed, "what's wrong? You can tell me."

"Nothing." She lowered her eyes. "Nothing's wrong. I'm considering my options, that's all."

"Well, consider this while you're at it. At least with me you won't have to worry about the bedroom door staying closed."

Refusing to admit how much his comment stung, Katherine met his eyes. "All right, Michael. I'll accept your application. But there are three more days of interviews scheduled and I'm committed to seeing the rest of the applicants."

Michael smiled. "When will I hear from you?"

"The first of next week I'll let you know, either way."

"Great." He stood and held out his hand. "I'm confident this will work."

She wished she could say the same. With a sinking sensation, she stood and fitted her hand to his.

After tossing her a cocky smile, he turned and walked away. Katherine watched him for a moment, then squared her shoulders and called the next number.

Katherine paused before the door that announced Michael's. She could do this, she assured herself. She could do this because she didn't love him anymore. Drawing a deep breath, she pushed the door open and stepped inside.

Midafternoon sun spilled through the picture windows at the far end of the otherwise dim room, creating a dramatic chiaroscuro reminiscent of a Rembrandt painting. Ceiling fans turned lazily overhead; staccato bursts of sudden laughter punctuated the musical flow of quiet conversations.

Katherine stood in the shadowed doorway, her eyes unwittingly glued to him, her mouth suddenly dry. Michael was behind the bar, gesturing broadly as he talked to a group of students. She shook her head, her inky hair rippling with the movement. Some things never changed. Michael had been a hit with the college crowd when they were at Northern together, and he was a hit with them now.

Setting her jaw, she crossed to the bar. "Hello, Michael."

He looked up and smiled. "Katherine. I wondered when I'd hear from you."

She stuffed her hands into the pockets of her white wool coat. "Well, today's Monday."

"Is the news good?" His smile widened.

She could tell by his smug expression that he already knew it was. Katherine silently swore. "One of my bigmouth students beat me here."

Michael laughed as he added Irish whiskey to a cup of coffee then topped it with whipped cream and a cherry. "You know what they say about a bartender being the next best thing to a priest."

"Well, I'll make it official then. Your application has been chosen..." Her words trailed off as she realized he'd made her favorite drink. In the next moment, she realized he'd remembered it, and her heart skipped a beat. "Oh, Michael, I only came in to...I don't have time..."

Michael set the drink, along with a packet of sugar, on the bar in front of her. "It's on the house."

Katherine felt her cheeks heat and cursed her fair skin. "Well, I guess I have time for one." Feeling awkward and more than a little silly, Katherine busied herself with unbuttoning her coat and pulling off her gloves.

"Just get out of class?" he asked, pouring himself a cup of coffee.

"Um-hmm." She slipped out of her coat, then sat down. Hooking her heels on the middle rung of the stool, she stirred the whipped cream into the coffee until it was nothing but a frothy layer on top of the cup.

"It's been a long time, hasn't it?"

Katherine lifted her head to find him staring at her. She shifted on her stool. "Since what?"

"Since we've been together."

Heat washed over her and she shifted again. "Yes, I guess it has."

Michael plucked a cocktail straw from the box behind the bar and chewed on its end. "We really had some good times."

Katherine tightened her grip on the cup. "Yeah, great." She took a sip of the hot, sweet liquid and almost choked.

"I'll never forget the time we got lost in Chicago trying to find the Museum of Natural History. You were so scared."

Katherine remembered a fear so strong she'd shaken for hours afterward. Michael had bluffed their way out of a serious situation and all she'd been able to do was cry. "I still can't believe you talked me into stopping at that bar for a drink! People disappear on the South Side of Chicago."

Michael grinned. "Everything turned out all right. It was an experience." He leaned on the edge of the bar, still chewing on his straw. "Have you gotten that close to a street gang since?"

"No, thank God."

Michael laughed. "Still the same serious, cautious little Katie, I see."

She lifted her chin defiantly. "Still the same reckless, irreverent Michael."

Not at all offended, he laughed again and leaned toward her. "Do you remember the time we went camping? That first night, it was so cold—"

"Yes, of course I do," Katherine interrupted briskly, wishing she didn't. How could she have forgotten? She remembered that camping trip as if it were yesterday, remembering both the biting cold, then the searing heat of Michael's body. "So—"

"I thought we'd freeze. Crazy kids." He shook his head, still smiling at the memory.

She'd been crazy, all right. Crazy in love with a guy who thought of her as a sweet kid and a good buddy. Her palms were damp and she wiped them against her thighs. Over the years, she'd futilely wished he'd never offered the warmth of his sleeping bag that night, had time and again regretted accepting his offer. The memory of sharing that warm cocoon with him, of the way he'd smelled of wood smoke and musk, of wanting him so badly she couldn't sleep, had haunted her ever since.

Feeling too vulnerable, Katherine scrambled for a change of subject. "Business looks good."

Michael shot her a questioning glance, then straightened up. "Yeah, it seems I'm the favorite hangout this week."

"Terrific." She knew her smile was too bright, and tried to soften its glint.

He tossed the mangled straw in the trash. "What's the next step?"

It took Katherine a moment to realize he was talking about the experiment. She shuddered—out of the frying pan and into the fire. "Wednesday night there's a group meeting for everyone participating in the experiment. At that time we'll be asked questions about our daily routines, attitudes, life-styles. You can move in anytime after that."

"Sounds good, Katie." He shoved his hands into the back pockets of his jeans. "Where and what time?"

Sounds good? she thought incredulously. It was her idea of a nightmare. Why couldn't one halfway-normal man have applied? "Seven-thirty at the Social Sciences building, room one-forty-one." She slid off the stool and grabbed her coat. "Thanks for the drink."

"Anytime, Katie. See you Wednesday."

She slipped into her coat and wound the thick white scarf around her neck. She lifted her hand in goodbye and, without a backward glance, hurried across the room.

A moment later she was out in the brittle February day. It was a welcome respite from the claustrophobia she'd begun to feel inside. The frigid air stung her overheated cheeks and cooled her sweat-dampened skin.

Her boots crunched against the loosely packed snow as she crossed to the car. After first fumbling with the keys, then the lock, she slipped inside.

Katherine took two long, steadying breaths. See, that wasn't so bad, she assured herself. She curled her fingers around the steering wheel at the lie. No, horrible was a much better description.

She started the car, then sat back while the engine warmed up. If only he hadn't brought up their shared past. The last thing she needed to be reminded of was her adolescent and unrequited crush on Michael Tardo.

The corner of her mouth lifted in wry amusement. That was something she had no problem remembering all on her own.

Two

They had met her first day at Northern. She'd been a freshman, more eager and more naive than most, determined that the next four years would be the most rewarding of her life. That morning she'd put on one of her new fall outfits and headed to the university bookstore, anxious to buy all her texts and supplies for the semester. The trip had taken most of the morning, and by the time she'd trudged back across the huge campus, she'd been hot, irritated and exhausted.

She remembered climbing the last flight of stairs to her floor, muttering under her breath all the way. What kind of university was this anyway? she'd wondered, feeling sweat trickle between her shoulder blades. How could you live in a high-rise dormitory with a broken elevator?

Her arms had quivered and her bangs had clung to her damp forehead. And why, she silently wailed, had she worn this stupid outfit? At eight in the morning it had seemed the perfect choice. But then, she hadn't taken the time to check the weather.

Katherine groaned and shifted the monumental weight of the textbooks. So, on a day when the temperature had risen to an unseasonable eighty degrees, she was wearing a wool sweater and corduroy pants and carrying a load that would have tested a frontline football player.

The stack of textbooks seemed to have tripled in weight by the time she reached her dorm-room door. Juggling them, she inched her fingers into her pockets for her keys and came up empty. She drew her eyebrows together in concern, readjusted the books and tried the other pocket. Nothing.

She'd forgotten her keys! How could she have done something so stupid? How? Katherine rested her forehead against the door and her heavy glasses slipped down her nose. Tears welled in her eyes. She couldn't carry these books one step farther. Not one step. But if she left them and went to get the dorm monitor, they might disappear. In a burst of frustration, she kicked the door.

"Need some help?"

At the male voice, Katherine looked over her shoulder and squinted, tipping her head back so she could see through her glasses.

The guy standing behind her reached over and pushed the glasses back up her nose. "Better?"

"Yes, tha—" Color flooded her cheeks as her world came back into focus—the guy standing behind her was gorgeous! Her gaze traveled from beautiful brown eyes to running shoes that were held together with electrical tape, then back up. He was wearing a pair of silky jogging shorts and a sleeveless, cutoff sweatshirt. The sweatshirt revealed an almost indecent expanse of his muscled belly, and she stared at the firm, tanned flesh.

Katherine realized what she was doing and jerked her gaze back to his face. Laughter danced in his sexy eyes, and she felt heat creep up her already burning cheeks. "I...um...I guess I forgot my keys. *You guess you forgot your keys? Great going, Katherine, now he'll think you're an idiot as well as a nerd.* She wanted to die.

"No problem." He plucked his student ID card from its resting place—the waistband of his shorts. He slipped the card into the crack between the door and the jamb, wiggled it a few times, and then she heard a click.

Her mouth dropped as the door swung open. "Where did you learn to do that?"

This time his gaze swept over her. The corners of his lips tipped up. "Trust me, little bit, you don't want to know." He took the stack of books from her arms as if they weighed nothing and carried them into the room.

Little bit? she thought indignantly. Who did he think she was, somebody's kid sister? And why wouldn't she want to know?

He set the books on the bed, then glanced around. "Yours looks just like mine."

Katherine stood uncertainly in the doorway. "Pardon?"

"Your room looks just like mine. I live down the hall." He hooked his thumbs in the waistband of his shorts. "I'm Michael Tardo."

"Hi..." She nervously folded her arms across her chest. "I'm Katherine Reed." He gazed at her for a moment, then smiled. The curving of his lips was slow and bold, and suddenly it seemed as if there wasn't enough air in the room. Light-headed, Katherine squeezed her eyes shut and took a deep breath.

"I see you take this college stuff seriously." He scanned the stack of texts. "*Introduction to Sociology*...English Literature...Western Civilization..." He turned and shot her an amused look. "Calculus? What is your major anyway?"

"I haven't decided yet, but I want to get the most out of my college experience. I thought I'd try a little of everything my first semester and...so..." Her words trailed off in embarrassment. His eyes had crinkled at the corners and it looked as if he were about to laugh. And who could blame him? She sounded like a little bookworm. Her heart sank. A guy like him would never be interested in a bookworm. "Well, thanks for the help."

"Anytime." He smiled again and sauntered to the door. He stopped just outside it and turned around. "We're having a party tonight. Room six-eighteen. Stop by if you can."

Katherine swallowed. "You're inviting me to a party?"

"Yeah. See you then, Katie."

Katie, she thought as sudden laughter jerked her out of her reverie. She gazed out the car window at a group of rowdy students on their way into the bar, then shook her head. That had been the beginning of her infatuation with Michael. Infatuation? More like love at first sight. Oh, she'd told herself all the things a serious, intellectual girl would at a time like that—she'd just met him, looks meant nothing, she wasn't his type. But the warnings had been too late. She'd fallen head over heels for a guy who would never love her back.

Her initial reactions had, over time, been proven correct. He never *had* fallen in love with her. She'd tried everything, but he'd never thought of her as more than a friend. Except for one night. One sweet, bitter, fateful night.

Katherine pushed that particular memory resolutely away. At least she could take satisfaction in knowing she was over the crush and that any romantic feelings she'd had for Michael Tardo had died long ago. What was left was only emotional residue.

Sure it was. Shifting the car into first, she headed out of the parking lot.

Wednesday night arrived with a speed that left Katherine breathless. She stepped from the car, then, oblivious to the cold, stood staring at the Social Sciences building for a long moment. Living with Michael...she wasn't sure she was up to it. All the bravado, all the blustery affirmations were just a lot of hot air. The truth was, she had the feeling she was making the second biggest mistake of her life.

Her wool coat was no competition for the winter wind, and Katherine burrowed deeper into its collar. Mistake or not, she was committed. Backing out now would only raise a lot of questions in Michael's mind, questions she wasn't prepared to answer. She smiled in wry amusement as she remembered the one that had gotten her into this mess in the first place—*why are you so opposed to this?*

Katherine squared her shoulders and headed across the parking lot. She would face this because she had to. And it would be okay. She would stay out of Michael's way, he would stay out of hers and everybody would be happy.

She climbed the steps slowly, then pulled open one of the double glass doors. The building was brightly lit and warm. Katherine pulled off her gloves and unwound her scarf as she walked down the hall. Excited conversation mingled with laughter greeted her, and she smiled. This year's grads were the best she could remember—enthusiastic, inquisitive, bright. Every class had stars, but this class had nothing *but* stars. They'd kept her on her toes since August—she chuckled to herself—and this experiment was just another example of their ingenuity.

Katherine stepped into the room, her smile dying on her lips. The students were sitting in a circle around Michael, listening raptly to one of his highly embellished, morally questionable stories. She drew her brows together as she recognized it. Irritated, she closed the door with more force than necessary.

At the sound, Michael looked up and smiled. It was one of his to-die-for smiles, all even, white teeth and dimples, and Katherine lifted her chin. "Hello, everybody." A collective—and rather sheepish—greeting went around the circle.

"Why don't we ask Dr. Reed," Michael said, standing. "Dr. Reed, in your expert opinion, was the behavior of the Big Bad Wolf sociopathic, psychopathic or merely antisocial?"

"I'm sure I don't know, Mr. Tardo. At this point I have insufficient data. For example, I know nothing about his social environment or culture. Depending on those things—"

"His behavior may be none of the above," Marilyn Fuss chimed in. "Depending on the mores of his social environment, his behavior could be normal rather than aberrant."

"Exactly," Katherine pronounced, nodding at her student. She turned back to Michael. "Does that answer your question, Mr. Tardo?"

"For the time being, Dr. Reed."

Michael's eyes sparkled with amusement and Katherine swore under her breath and looked away. "Marilyn, are we ready to begin?"

"Let's wait another five minutes," Marilyn answered, consulting her clipboard. "We're missing three participants." When Katherine nodded, she called out, "Okay, everybody, we'll start in five."

From the corner of her eye, Katherine saw Michael whisper something to one of the coeds. She turned her back on him, but not before hearing the coed giggle in response. Katherine gritted her teeth. Well, she could see he still went for the same type of woman—blond, buxom and flashy. At least in college he'd dated women his own age. That girl was young enough—

"Sharp as ever," Michael murmured in her ear. "But watch out, Dr. Reed. Someday I'll catch you off guard."

For one brief moment Katherine's senses were flooded with him—his fresh, soapy scent, the cadence of his breathing, the warmth emanating from his body, so close to hers. She pushed the sensations away and spun around. "You and I need to have a conversation."

"Oh?" Michael lifted his eyebrows. "What about?"

"About the story you were telling when I walked in, for one thing. I wasn't amused."

Michael's jaw tightened. "Of course you weren't. Serious, straight-as-an-arrow Katherine wouldn't find a slightly off-color story amusing."

She curled her fingers into her palms and glared up at him. "And I don't know why I expected a little decorum from a man who wore jogging shorts to the Dean's reception."

He smiled wickedly. "I could have worn a lampshade. Or worse, nothing at all."

She stared at him for a moment, fighting the smile that tugged at her mouth. She gave in and laughed. "I suppose you're right."

Michael reached over and lightly chucked her on the chin. "Of course I am."

Katherine found the gesture unsettling in its intimacy, infuriating in its implication—he still thought of himself as a big brother. She stiffened her spine. "Michael, I know I overreacted a moment ago, but try to understand, I'm walking a fine line with this thing. If the wrong person had come through that door, this experiment might have been cancelled."

His smile faded. "I hadn't thought of that. Sorry, Katie. From now on, no more stories. And I promise not to wear lampshades—or worse—to any of the meetings."

"Thank you," Katherine murmured as Marilyn called everyone to order. She took a seat, mulling over what she'd said to Michael. Her concern over the experiment and the need for scholarly appearances was exaggerated. Michael's bawdy story or the chance that the wrong person could have heard it hadn't been responsible for her outburst. No, around Michael she felt vulnerable and awkward because she couldn't forget, even for a moment, their past or the shy, nerdy girl she'd been. And feeling those things set her teeth on edge.

How was she going to share her home and all the intimacies of day-to-day life with him, if she couldn't even handle sharing the public arena of a classroom? She could only hope that as time passed she would become desensitized to his presence in her life.

With a sigh, Katherine shifted her attention to the front of the room. Marilyn had begun to speak.

"...glad you could all be here. I'm Marilyn Fuss and this is my husband, Ron. Because we can't participate in the experiment, we'll be conducting the weekly interviews, compiling and interpreting the data and generally overseeing the groups. If you have any problems or questions, feel free to..."

Katherine's gaze wandered across to Michael. He was sprawled comfortably in a chair, his long legs stretched out in front of him. His eyes were directed to the front of the room; his lids were partially lowered, giving him a look of lazy attentiveness.

But she knew Michael Tardo too well; he was bored to tears. Michael needed action. He needed fresh air or smoky bars, loud music or lots of laughter. He'd never been suited to a classroom—she should know, she'd covered for him when he cut class more times than she could remember—he'd always found the academic atmosphere suffocating. As Marilyn coughed and cleared her throat, her attention flew back to the front of the room.

"Sociology is the study of human behavior. We believe that behavior is shaped largely by the groups to which people belong and by the social interaction that takes place in those groups. Therefore..."

Katherine's gaze crept back to Michael. It looked as if he were doodling on the paper in front of him. She sighed. Michael would never change. He would always be the bad boy of the cool crowd, always the first one with a joke and the last one to leave a party. With a small shake of her head, she returned her focus to Marilyn and Ron.

"The social scientist looks for behavioral patterns. In this case we believe, and are attempting to prove, that there's a predictable relationship between cohabitation and behavior we usually type 'married.' Once a pattern is established we'll attempt to prove the correlation between..."

Katherine dared another peek at Michael. He'd shifted in his seat, and his fingers drummed a tune on his thigh. He wore the same faded black jeans as the other night; his thick wool sweater was also black. Her eyes trailed slowly upward across his broad chest and shoulders to rest on his mouth. As she watched, it curved slightly, as if from an amusing secret, and she jerked her gaze away.

"...surveyed a random sample of people to determine what qualities, or behavioral characteristics, they considered those of married couples. The results of that survey should define 'married' behavior in our society, and are the qualities we'll be monitoring you for." Marilyn shoved her glasses back up her nose. "Of course, we can't reveal the results of the survey without running the risk of influencing your behavior either in support or denial of our theory. From this point we'll..."

Michael stifled a yawn. Why did scientists—social or otherwise—have to be so damn boring? Why couldn't they simply and quickly explain what the deal was, then get on with it? At the rate things were going, he would be here all night.

His gaze strayed to Katherine. Tonight she looked more like one of the students than the professor. Her hair was pulled back in a loose ponytail; feathery wisps escaped their confinement and framed her face. He cocked his head as he studied her. Maybe the virginal white she wore added to the illusion of youth. Or maybe it was the way the bulky sweater acted as a foil for her delicacy, or the way the garment's soft, fuzzy fabric contrasted with the smooth perfection of her skin.

Michael smiled to himself. He still wasn't used to seeing her without her glasses. The first time they'd met those glasses had been balancing on the very tip of her nose, and she'd been squinting to make him out. He'd pushed them back up then and a hundred times after. Tonight, he'd reached out to do the same, and they hadn't been there.

He shook his head, remembering the day they'd met. She'd been disheveled and flustered; he'd made a crack about the size of her books compared to the size of her. Even through her thick lenses he'd seen her eyes snap as she'd pinned him with her volatile gaze and said, "Small stature, big brain." He'd understood right away that Katherine Reed couldn't be swayed by a quick grin or a handsome face.

So they'd become friends. She'd helped him through classes, had listened to his dreams when everyone else expected jokes, had lectured him on the merits of both study and sobriety. For his part, he'd introduced her to people she would otherwise have been too introverted to meet, had gotten her invited to the best parties, had made her laugh when she was sad.

Michael's smile faded. That had all ended in their senior year. One day everything had been fine, the next she'd been cool and reserved. Who could blame her? He'd gotten drunk and come pounding on her door for help once too often.

Every time he thought about his past and the person he'd been during those years, regret washed over him. He'd been out of control; so afraid he was like his no-good father that he'd done everything in his power to be just that. He shook his head. It was funny. He'd been running straight toward the thing he feared most.

He lifted his eyes once again to Katherine's face. He'd missed her friendship more than he would have thought possible. He hadn't expected to ache for her smile at the oddest times and for no reason at all. Nor had he expected loneliness or the bittersweet quality of remembering.

Of course, back then he'd thought himself tough, cool, invincible; he'd thought he didn't need anybody—especially a shy little bookworm. And as he'd often been during those years, he'd been wrong.

About a year ago, he had learned she was in town, teaching at the college. He'd wanted to look her up; a dozen times he'd started to, but he never had. And he wasn't sure why.

Now they were going to live together. Michael shook his head as he drew a series of meaningless shapes on the edge of his paper. Originally he'd thought this whole venture would be a breeze. Now he wasn't so sure. Her anger of minutes before had reminded him that she used to get mad at him a lot. He swallowed a laugh. She would get annoyed over one of his crazy, irresponsible stunts; he'd egg her on by laughing or teasing; she would end up spitting mad and lecturing him on whatever it was she considered he'd done wrong. Funny thing was, eventually she'd lectured some sense into him. With another shake of his head, he looked back up at Marilyn.

"After this evening, you'll meet with us once a week, at times with your partner, at times independently. Ron and I will ask you about your week, about your feelings for your partner and so on. We'll evaluate your response according to the information you give us tonight. For the study to be valid, you must be absolutely frank with us." Marilyn glanced back down at her clipboard of notes. "Some of you are being supplied with living areas available in the married dorms. Others of you have adequate housing off campus. Either way, remember to stick to your normal routine as closely as possible."

"That's right," Ron said, clearing his throat. "In addition, I know some of you are having trouble getting your steadies to understand what we're doing. See me before you leave and I'll set up a time to meet with them and try to make some assurances. Are there any questions?"

There weren't, and the rest of the meeting flew by in a flurry of filling out forms and answering questions. By the time the session broke up at ten-thirty, Katherine was exhausted. After a round of goodbyes, she slipped into her coat and headed toward the door.

"I'll walk you to your car," Michael said, falling in step beside her.

She shot him a glance from the corner of her eyes. "That's not necessary. I don't need protecting."

"I know. But I want to."

"I guess I can't argue with that."

"Nope." His eyes crinkled at the corners. "Not without being rude, anyway."

They were silent as they stepped outside into the cold, black night. Neither spoke as they crossed the parking lot, and Katherine was achingly aware of him beside her. Once when she slipped, he steadied her with a hand on her elbow, and she thought her heart would fly out of her chest, it was beating so fast.

When they finally reached her car, Katherine breathed a small sigh of relief. "Here it is," she said, pulling out her keys and meeting his eyes. "Thank you. I appreciate your escorting me."

"Anytime." He didn't move.

Her pulse fluttered. "Well . . . good night."

"It doesn't have to be," he murmured.

The blood rushed to her head. "Excuse me?"

"It doesn't have to be good-night. We could have coffee, or hit a late show and a diner after."

Longing, so poignant her chest ached, washed over her. *Yes* rushed to her lips; she choked back the word a moment before she uttered it. Feeling hot and flustered, she cleared her throat and tried to act normally. "I'm very tired, Michael. I have an early class and—"

"No problem, Katie." He touched her lightly on the nose with his index finger. "Your nose is cold."

"Yes."

"I thought I'd move in Saturday."

The breathlessness was back; she swallowed past it. "Fine," she murmured, fumbling with the keys.

"Let me." He plucked them from her fingers, unlocked and opened the door.

Katherine slipped inside and busied herself with starting the car and fastening her safety belt. When she'd run out of things to do, she looked back up at him. "Well . . . I guess I'll see you Saturday."

"I guess you will." He smiled down at her as he shut the car door. With a quick wave, he turned and walked away.

Katherine watched him go, feeling as if she'd just tiptoed through an emotional mine field. With a small sigh, she headed home.

Three

At six o'clock Saturday morning Katherine's eyes flew open, and she knew more sleep was only a sweet dream. She rolled onto her side and closed her eyes anyway, then groaned as a picture of Michael floated on the back of her eyelids.

This was crazy, she thought with a frown. Why couldn't she put him out of her mind? They hadn't spent time together in eight years. And in those eight years, she'd only thought of him . . . every day, she finished, cursing her own honesty.

Frustrated, Katherine tossed aside the covers and climbed out of bed. After yanking on her robe, she headed to the kitchen to make coffee. She could handle living with Michael, she thought fiercely, slamming the cupboard door. She spooned coffee into the filter basket, shoved the pot onto its burner, then flipped the switch on. They had nothing in common; he would probably bore her silly. Sure he would.

Then why was she so rattled? With another groan, she stalked to the bathroom to shower.

Michael's knock came at twelve minutes after one. Katherine sprang up from the couch and the magazine in her lap hit the floor with a sharp slap. She smoothed her black wool slacks, picked up the magazine and took a deep breath. She'd been on pins and needles since she stepped out of her morning shower, vacillating between wanting to call the whole thing off and being determined to see it through. Determination had won. Squaring her shoulders, she crossed to the door.

"Hi..." The greeting died on her lips. He was holding a huge bouquet of long-stemmed red roses. Warmth eased up her spine. Michael had brought her flowers.

"Hello to you, too." He held out the bouquet. "Happy Valentine's Day, I guess."

With trembling hands, Katherine took the arrangement. She buried her face in the blossoms. Their subtly sweet scent filled her head. "They're wonderful," she murmured. "But you shouldn't have."

He bent to retrieve a box of half-dead plants. "I didn't. The card's there."

"The card?" she repeated.

He shrugged. "Yeah. I met the delivery boy at the door. Where can I put these?"

Delivery boy? They weren't from...he'd let her think... Her cheeks heated. Would she ever stop acting the fool over Michael Tardo? "Anywhere," she muttered, setting the flowers on the brass-and-glass entryway table. She plucked the card from its resting place, but didn't open it.

Her gaze skimmed over him as he deposited his box of plants next to the bouquet. His hair was still rumpled from sleep; there was a long crease on his right cheek where his face had been crushed into a pillow. He'd just gotten up, she thought, instantly annoyed. She'd been crawling the walls since six o'clock; he'd been enjoying a peaceful sleep—and probably not alone. Katherine gritted her teeth. Michael would never change.

He hauled in two suitcases and a garment bag, then dropped them onto the thick white carpeting. "Aren't you going to open it?"

"What?" When he motioned, she looked down at the card clutched in her hand. Annoyed with herself, she pulled the small, plain card out of the envelope.

Say yes. Dean.

Michael peered over her shoulder. "Say yes to what?"

"Excuse me?" Katherine shot him a frosty glance.

"The card."

A choice expletive sprang to her lips; she swallowed it. History was not going to repeat itself, she decided resolutely. "I know what you meant," she said, slipping the card back into its envelope. "That was a polite way of telling you to mind your own business." She tucked the card into her pocket. "Would you like a cup of coffee?"

Michael cocked an eyebrow. Katherine had changed. Eight years ago she wouldn't have let that pass. Her cheeks and eyes would have heated, and she would have shot back an indignant reply that would have led to a shouting match. Today she hadn't even blinked. He shook off a vague disappointment. "I'd love one."

Katherine led him to the kitchen, trying to ignore the trail of garments he left in his wake: gloves on the couch, scarf on the bar and finally, his coat thrown over the back of a kitchen chair. Drawing a slow breath, she resisted the urge to go back and pick each one up. How could she have forgotten what a slob Michael was? His dorm room had always been total chaos.

She took two cups from the cupboard, then crossed to the coffeepot. "Still take it black?"

"Uh-huh." He smiled and met her eyes. "Still take it sweet?"

A lump formed in her throat. He'd teased her once that she would never find a lover as sweet as she took her coffee. But she had—once. Her fingers shook as she spooned sugar into the cup, and she cursed under her breath.

"You have a nice place." He leaned against the counter and folded his arms across his chest. "But I'm not surprised. You always preferred nice things."

Except when it came to men, Katherine thought. Then her taste ran to dark, wild and dangerous. Even now, with his mussed hair and sleepy eyes, he was the most appealing man she'd ever known. She handed him his coffee. "Come on, I'll show you around."

"Great." For the next few minutes, Michael followed her, listening as she pointed out where the clean linen was kept and explained how to use the washer and dryer. Decorated in whites and creams, her home was tasteful and serene. But as in Katherine herself, there were hints of fire: the shocking-pink pillows on the white couch, the African ceremonial mask in the otherwise stark bathroom, the huge, wildly colored dried-flower arrangement in the hallway.

Michael shook his head. Yes, Katherine liked nice things. Her cultured mother and father had been quick to point that out the first time they'd met him. They'd also made it clear they didn't approve of their daughter's friendship with the likes of Michael Tardo.

"This is my... bedroom."

She cleared her throat and pulled the door shut, but not before he'd gotten a good look at the large, blatantly feminine room. Michael smiled. She was obviously embarrassed to have him see it. A surge of warmth and protectiveness washed over him. Katie had always been sweet and shy with men. It looked as if some things about her hadn't changed.

"Here's your room. There's plenty of closet and drawer space, but if you need..." She glanced over her shoulder at Michael and the words died on her tongue. The softest smile played about his lips and the expression in his eyes was tender—almost loving. Her chest tightened and she looked away. She would never make it through the next eight weeks if she started imagining loving glances and tender smiles. She'd bought into that madness eight years ago and all it had gotten her was a broken heart.

"Nice," Michael said, his eyes lingering on the gentle curve of her cheek. "Mind if I get unpacked?"

Firming her resolve, Katherine turned and faced him. She couldn't quite meet his eyes and silently swore. "No, go ahead. I've got some work to do. You just do... whatever."

"Don't worry about me, I'll be out of your way shortly." He checked his watch. "I'm meeting someone at three."

He had a date. There was a sinking sensation in the pit of her stomach; she ignored it. "Oh. Well . . . you'll probably want to clean up before you go. Make yourself at home. If you need anything, I'll be in my study."

"Thanks." He smiled. "Look, Katherine, before we get into this, are there any idiosyncrasies that set your teeth on edge? I'd rather prevent gunfire than dodge it. We used to have a pretty volatile relationship."

Just having him here was enough to set her whole nervous system on edge. As for fireworks, she was going to try her best to remain as unemotional as possible. "No," Katherine answered as they began walking back to the entryway. "The purpose of this experiment is to evaluate any changes in your normal behavior pattern as a result of cohabitation. It would invalidate the conclusions if I made you conform to my likes and dislikes."

Michael shrugged and crossed to his suitcases. "Okay. But I won't be easy to live with."

Where did he get the flare for understatement? she wondered, watching as he carried his suitcases back down the hall. And who was he meeting this afternoon? Scowling at her thoughts, she slipped into her study and closed the door behind her.

Michael heard the vigorous rock and roll even before he reached the door and raised his brows—rock was hardly Katherine's favorite music. If he remembered correctly, her tastes ran more to Chopin and Debussy. He pulled out his key, opened the door and stepped inside. Maybe this was another of her students' experiments—something like a study to evaluate the behavioral effects of listening to abhorrent music.

His thoughts came to an abrupt halt as he entered the living room. Katherine was in front of the television, stretching and bending in time with a workout tape.

Michael swallowed—hard. She was wearing a lilac-colored bit of spandex, cut high on the hip. Unbearably so, he thought, watching as she slowly bent until her palms rested on the floor. He released a long breath when she straightened, only to catch it again when she arched her back and reached for the ceiling.

Michael slipped a finger under his suddenly snug turtleneck. Katherine's exposed back was wet with sweat and looked silky-smooth. He imagined his hands sliding over the glistening flesh, absorbing her heat, molding her to him, and his mouth went dry. He would press his lips to the curve between her neck and shoulder and taste—

Michael shook his head and jerked his gaze away. This was Katherine, for God's sake. This was his Katie, the woman who'd stood by him even when he acted like a class-A jerk. Dammit, she was his friend. They'd even shared a sleeping bag . . .

And he hadn't slept all night, he recalled, almost groaning out loud as the memory filled his head.

"I—I'm . . . fr-freezing," she'd whispered, her teeth chattering.

Michael remembered looking over at her. She was huddled inside the sleeping bag, with only her nose and eyes visible. A surge of protectiveness had gone through him as he thought what a ridiculously small form she made, even with the added bulk of the bag. "Me, too," he'd whispered back. "I'm sorry I got you into this."

"It's not y-your fault." Her blue eyes filled with tears. "If only we could have a fire."

"It's too windy." Even as he spoke, the wind screamed through the trees.

"I kn-know. But m-maybe we could hike back to the car?" Her voice lifted hopefully.

"No way, Katie. It's too far, and I'm not even sure I could find the way in the dark." When a single tear rolled down her cheek, a lump formed in his throat. She was so small and sweet, and he'd subjected her to this. "Why don't you come over here and share my bag? Our combined body heat will keep us warm."

He didn't have to ask twice. She scrambled up and within moments, was snuggled against him. At first it was still bitterly cold, but then slowly, heat began to creep over them. Her back was pressed against him and his chin rested on the top of her head. She smelled like baby powder and lilacs. He breathed deeply and the scent, at once innocent and alluring, raced over his senses.

"Feel better, Katie?" he asked, his voice soft and thick.

"Yes," she murmured sleepily. "Thank you, Michael."

She yawned and shifted. As she did, her hips first brushed, then settled against his manhood. Arousal was instantaneous and overpowering. Before he realized what he was doing, he wrapped his arms around her and pulled her even closer. Michael immediately knew he'd made a mistake. Now, instead of just her hips, her whole, perfect body was pressed against his. God, she felt as if she'd been made for him.

Breathing deeply through his nose, Michael reminded himself that this was Katie, his friend. He told himself she trusted him, and tried to picture the way she'd looked last month when she had the flu. Nothing lessened the ache of arousal, and he squeezed his eyes shut. How was he going to get to sleep now?

He *hadn't* gotten any sleep, Michael remembered. In fact he'd remained hot, restless and awake the whole night. The next morning, frustrated and exhausted, he'd snapped at Katherine so many times she'd gotten hurt and refused to speak to him for the rest of the day.

Michael groaned as he looked back at Katherine—she was doing something with her hips that was proving lethal to his sanity. Eight years ago he must have had a lot more control than he did today, he thought, a knot of desire tightening in his belly. If she crawled into a sleeping bag with him now, he didn't think he could let her go until she'd been thoroughly loved.

"So, that's how you keep your fanny so pert," he said, forcing lightness into his tone.

Katherine whirled around, color flooding her cheeks. "What are you doing here?"

"I live here." He unzipped his down vest and shrugged out of it. "You haven't forgotten, have you?" He shot her a quick, lopsided grin.

"Yes...no, I meant, I didn't expect to...I haven't seen you all week," she finished, then silently swore. Could she have any less grace? "Besides, you should know better than to sneak up on people."

Michael laughed softly. "And you should think about turning the music down."

He had her there. The truth was, she hadn't expected to see him. Their paths hadn't crossed since the day he'd moved in. When she was getting ready to leave for work, he was sleeping; when he got in at night, she was sleeping. Except for the evidence of his presence—traces of his morning shave in the sink, his shampoo in the shower, fast-food wrappers in the trash—Katherine could almost believe she still lived alone. Crossing to the VCR, she started rewinding the tape.

"Don't let me interrupt your workout," Michael said, smiling wickedly and tossing the ski vest on a chair. "I'll just watch."

A tart reply sprang to her lips; she choked it back. She wouldn't take the bait, Katherine told herself. She would remain cool and unaffected. Feigning nonchalance, she glanced over her shoulder at him. "Sorry, Michael, the show's over." She ejected the tape, slipped it into its case, then headed toward the back of the house. "Oh, in case you're gone when I get out of the shower, have a nice time tonight."

She smiled to herself as she closed the bathroom door behind her. Well, that hadn't been so bad after all. All week she'd been dreading the moment when she and Michael would come face to face again. She turned on the water to warm it up and began peeling off her damp leotard and tights. Even though he'd surprised her in such an embarrassing position, she'd kept her cool. This living-together thing might not be so bad after all. Humming to herself, she stepped under the hot, stinging spray.

Twenty minutes later, Katherine was still smiling as she headed for the kitchen. Her stomach rumbled. On Friday nights she had a favorite ritual—first an aerobic workout, then cooking something complicated and fattening. Tonight she was trying a seafood frittata; it would be either interesting—or poisonous.

"Have a nice shower?"

Katherine spun around, her smile fading. Michael was sprawled comfortably on her white sofa. He'd kicked off his shoes and tossed all the throw pillows but the one under his head to the floor. The magazines on the coffee table, which had been arranged in a neat fan, were now in a jumble. And he looked comfortable—too comfortable. Surely he didn't plan to stay?

"Why haven't you left?" she asked, not caring that she sounded ungracious.

Michael didn't answer, but instead let his eyes trail slowly over her. She wore a gray fleece sweatsuit and bright blue sweat socks. Her hair was piled on top of her head and held with a big silver clip. Strands, still damp from her shower, clung to her flushed cheeks and the elegant line of her neck. As she reached up to brush them away from her face, he thought of a lilac-colored leotard and white, wet skin.

He met her eyes. "I'm not going out."

Katherine's breath caught. "Pardon?" Maybe she'd misunderstood him. Maybe—

"I decided to hang around." The truth was, he'd had plans—and changed them.

Her heart sank. "Oh . . . well, fine. After all, you live here, too."

He grinned up at her. "Thanks for the concession, Katie. I was beginning to feel unwanted."

He looked like a naughty little boy, and a smile tugged at her mouth. She shook her head. "Do whatever you want, Michael. I'll be in the kitchen." Without another word, she turned and headed that way.

He jumped up and followed her. "What are we making?"

"We?" she asked, arching an eyebrow.

He laughed. "Yeah, we."

She opened the refrigerator and took out the butter, eggs and cream, then shot him an amused glance. "I thought your taste ran more to meals packed in Styrofoam."

"So I have a thing for Styrofoam. Sue me."

"Tempting," she murmured, taking a container of seafood from the freezer.

Tempting was right, he thought, eyeing the patch of creamy skin that was exposed at her midriff as she stood on tiptoe to reach a high shelf. If he were a gentleman, he'd offer to help. His lips curved as he acknowledged that he wasn't. "What's in the container?"

"Scallops, shrimp and crab." Katherine set several jars of spices on the counter. "I'm making a seafood frittata." She turned on the hot water, dumped the seafood into a colander and set it under the stream of water.

He leaned against the counter. "Which is—?"

"A fancy omelet," she answered, smiling. "How are you at making salads. There's some romaine in the fridge."

"Does this mean I'm invited to stay?" he asked, already rummaging in the vegetable bin. He didn't expect an answer and she didn't give him one. While she worked on the frittata, he made himself at home, searching through cupboards and drawers until he found the salad bowl and utensils.

After many minutes of companionable silence, he heard a muffled oath and glanced at Katherine from the corner of his eye. She'd spilled flour and the saucepan was smoking. He smiled as she simultaneously reached for the smoking pan with one hand, burning herself, and pushed the hair away from her face with the other, leaving a long white streak on her cheek. Saying she wasn't comfortable in the kitchen would be an understatement. Saying this whole frittata thing might be a bust would be closer to the truth.

He shook his head and crumbled blue cheese on top of the salad. She wouldn't take kindly to an offer of help. Not that his offer would be much good—she'd been right, his mealtime experience ran more to Styrofoam and drive-through windows.

"This isn't working," she muttered, frustrated. "The shrimp is supposed to turn pink. Is this pink?"

Michael looked over her shoulder. His stomach rolled. "That's shrimp?"

"And these eggs are supposed to rise." She pushed at the flat, rubbery mass with a spatula and groaned. "The recipe said this was an easy dish. I hate gourmet magazines. They always lie."

Michael bit back a laugh as she swiped at her other cheek and left another flour mark. "How about a glass of wine?"

"God, yes."

There was a bottle of white Zinfandel in the refrigerator. He poured two glasses, setting one on the counter next to her.

"Thanks," she said, not looking up.

Her head was bent as she concentrated on turning the eggs. His eyes lowered to, then lingered on, the nape of her neck. The skin looked soft, vulnerable and all too inviting. He reached out to touch her, then realized what he was doing and dropped his hand. "You know," he murmured, "in all the years we've been friends, we've never cooked a meal together. Unless you count about a hundred peanut-butter-and-banana sandwiches."

"And do you wonder why?" she asked, motioning toward the saucepan and its unappetizing gray contents. "I don't know what I did wrong. I followed the directions... I'm sure I did." She glanced up at him, totally exasperated.

"Have you tasted it?" At the look on her face, he laughed. "Okay, I'll be the guinea pig. After all, how bad could it be?" He cautiously dipped a spoon in the sauce, then held it to his lips. The taste was a cross between hell and gruel, and his eyes began to water. He grabbed his glass and took a long, palate-cleansing sip of wine.

"It's awful, isn't it?" Katherine clasped her hands in front of her.

"I wouldn't say 'awful.'" He took another sip of the wine, this time sloshing it around his mouth before swallowing.

"What would you say?"

"Well..." Michael gave her a sympathetic glance. "Anthony's Pizza delivers."

"Oh." Katherine sighed and sagged against the counter.

"We could go out," he suggested.

"I'm too hungry."

"Anthony's?"

"Takes too long." Her stomach growled. "It's already eight-thirty."

The last had bordered on a whine and Michael grinned. She looked adorable... and was feeling sorry for herself. Katherine had always gotten grumpy when she was hungry. Grumpy, then mean. He had better get her food, fast. A smile lit his face as he thought of just the thing.

Minutes later, they carried their wine and peanut-butter-and-banana sandwiches into the living room. He'd made them on thick slices of white bakery bread and garnished each plate with a handful of corn chips.

"This is a disgusting combination," Katherine murmured, taking a huge bite of her sandwich.

"No—" Michael popped a corn chip into his mouth "—what's disgusting is still in the kitchen."

It was an effort to keep from laughing out loud while her mouth was full. After she'd managed to swallow, she said, "I haven't had one of these in years."

"You used to love them."

She wiped her mouth with a napkin. "I think I still do."

They ate in silence and in no time at all had polished off the sandwiches and chips. Katherine curled her legs under her and sighed in contentment. "Delicious. I was starving."

"I could tell." He refilled their glasses, then leaned back against the couch. He stared at the delicately colored liquid for a moment, then back at her. "I used to wonder about you . . . where you were, what you were doing."

A lump formed in her throat, and Katherine looked away. "Oh."

He rolled the wineglass between his palms. "I even wrote you a couple of times."

Her eyes snapped back to his in surprise. "You did?"

"You never got them." Michael laughed without humor. "I didn't know how to reach you, so I sent them to your parents' house."

All these years she'd thought Michael had forgotten her. All these years she'd believed their friendship had meant nothing to him. And her parents had known differently. Anger was upon her so quickly, her voice shook with it. "I'm sorry, I didn't—"

"You didn't know," he finished for her, shrugging. "I figured. They never liked me, and I knew I was taking my chances when I wrote you in care of them."

"They had no right to screen my mail," she said tightly. "No right to decide who I should and shouldn't talk to."

He reached over and lightly touched her hair. It was as soft as mink under his fingers. He enjoyed the sensation for a moment, then regretfully dropped his hand. "Don't be angry with them. They had every reason to dislike me...I wasn't the type of guy a girl brought home to meet her parents. Not a nice girl, anyway."

Hot denial jumped to her lips; she swallowed it as she realized what she was doing. Eight years ago she'd passionately defended Michael to everyone, including her parents and Michael himself. Love had blinded her to his faults; it seemed nothing had changed.

Katherine glanced at him from the corner of her eyes. He was staring straight ahead; a muscle worked in his jaw. She knew what he was thinking, and her heart went out to him—no one had ever been as hard on Michael as he'd been on himself. To hell with pride, she couldn't *not* comfort him.

Katherine placed her hand over his. "You were a good friend to me, Michael," she said, wishing she could steady her voice. "You were always there, and you always cared." It was true. He hadn't been to blame for her pain. She was the one who'd complicated things, the one who'd asked for something that he couldn't give.

"Thank you," Michael murmured. "It's important for me to know you were able to count on me." He looked away, then back. "After my father...ran out on me and Mom, I promised myself I'd never let anyone down like that."

Poor Michael, Katherine thought, eyeing his tight expression. He'd made himself an impossible promise. There were people who would be disappointed no matter how hard he tried.

"He died about a year ago. I went to the funeral, but—" Michael paused "—I didn't feel any grief."

"Oh, Michael..."

"It's okay." He lifted her hand to his lips and placed a light kiss on her knuckles. "I like to think I've come to terms with what my father was...what he did. I didn't feel any grief, but I didn't feel any anger, either."

"I'm glad," she said, her voice husky.

"Me, too." He laced his fingers with hers. Her hand was small and soft in his, and he smiled. Being with Katherine had always felt good—comforting and somehow right. He suddenly realized how he'd missed that feeling. "You know, this is the first time we've talked in eight years."

Katherine stared at their joined hands, her mouth dry. She couldn't seem to form a coherent thought, so she remained silent.

"We used to talk so much. Remember the times we talked all night?"

"Mmm." Her pulse fluttered as he began softly stroking the back of her hand with his thumb.

"What have you been doing the past eight years, Katherine?"

What could she say? Reliving every moment they'd spent together and futilely wishing they'd never met or that things had worked out? When she thought back over those years, that was all that came to mind.

"Graduate school," she answered. "My doctorate, the teaching position."

"That's not what I mean." He trailed his thumb over the back of her wrist and imagined the translucent flesh throbbing under his touch. He pushed the image away. "I envisioned you married to some nice guy. A guy as smart and serious as you are. I thought you'd have a kid, maybe two." He released her hand but not her gaze. "Why haven't you?"

That he could so blithely picture her married with children was like a slap in the face. To cover her hurt, she reached for her wine and sipped it. It was cool, dry and soothing, and she held it against her tongue for a moment before swallowing. When she trusted her voice, she murmured, "I could ask you the same question."

He watched as she tipped her head to drink. Her neck arched and his eyes lingered. If he pressed his lips to the place where her pulse beat wildly at the base of her throat, would she smell of baby powder and lilacs? Even as he wondered, he dragged his thoughts back to her question. "Marrying has never even been an option." He downed the last of his wine and set aside the glass. "How about you? Ever wanted to take that big step?"

Katherine lowered her eyes. "Yes," she said softly. "Once, a long time ago."

Michael wasn't sure if he had heard the pain in her voice or just sensed it, but he knew that she'd been deeply hurt. "Wh—" His throat closed over the words, and he coughed to clear it "—what happened."

She picked up her glass, then realizing it was already empty, set it back down. "He didn't love me the same way."

The graduate student she'd dated their last year of school, Michael thought with certainty. He flexed his fingers as the urge to wring the man's neck surged through him. He'd never understood what she'd seen in that wimp.

Pushing away the emotion, he touched the curve of her cheek. Her skin was too inviting, and he feathered his fingers across the smooth, warm flesh. When she lifted her face into the caress, he caught his breath. "He was crazy. You're a prize."

Katherine raised her eyes to his and her pulse scrambled. His were soft, dark and mesmerizing. She shook her head, unsure whether in denial of his words or of his effect on her.

"Yes." He slid his hand into her hair. It was silky against his skin and to prolong the sensation, he combed his fingers through the gossamer strands for a moment before cupping her neck. "A prize."

Her breath shuddered past her lips. His touch and words were hypnotic and when he applied the tiniest pressure with his fingers, she leaned willingly toward him.

"Couldn't he see what I do?" he asked, lowering his eyes to her mouth. "You're loyal . . . talented . . ."

Katherine brought her hands to his chest and curled her fingers into his loosely woven sweater. He was so close she could see the tiny gold flecks in his eyes and feel his breath against her parted lips. He smelled of some spicy soap and the fruity wine. The combination was heady, and she inched even closer.

"And so lovely . . ."

He meant to kiss her, Katherine thought, heart thundering in her chest. She should push him away and demand an apology. If their lips met, he would know how she felt about him.

All the logical reasons why she should refuse him raced from her mind. They were replaced by a need so strong as to be overpowering. With a small sound of pleasure, she parted her lips, waiting for his touch.

She would taste sweet, feel wonderful against him. Michael gathered her closer. As he did, the scent of baby powder and lilacs enveloped him. What was he doing? he wondered. How could it be that he wanted her so badly he ached?

He didn't know or care; he only felt. Dazed, unnerved, he reached up and unfastened the clip in her hair and the midnight strands tumbled to her shoulders.

At the same moment he tangled his fingers in the thick, soft mass, an image of his mother's face, ravaged by pain, popped into his head. He'd only been six the night his father had walked out, but the image was as vivid as if it had been yesterday.

Katie. Michael opened his eyes. Hers were tightly closed and she looked incredibly fragile. A knot formed in his chest. He had assured her she would be safe if he was her partner. He'd promised her the bedroom door would stay closed. And now, at the first opportunity, he was seducing her. Some things seemed to run in the family.

Feeling like the boy he'd been at eighteen instead of the man he had become, the man he wanted to be, he took a shaky breath. If only she wasn't so soft and yielding against him. He tightened his fingers in her hair in denial. He and Katherine were just friends...they would stay that way. He couldn't chance anything else.

Gathering all his self-control, Michael relaxed his fingers and pushed her away. She made a sound of resistance as he did, and he silently groaned. Why did she have to be so damn sweet?

He dropped his hand as her lids fluttered up. Her blue eyes were stormy with need, and Michael realized if he didn't leave her now, he might not be able to. He stood up before she'd even dropped her hands from his chest. "It's been a hell of a week," he said, making a show of stretching and yawning. "I don't know about you, but I'm beat. Good night, Katie."

Four

———

Feeling numb, Katherine stared at the place where Michael had been only a moment ago. She realized she still had her hands lifted, as if she were holding him, and dropped them. She stood and started down the hallway to her own bedroom.

Moonlight bathed the room in cool blue and, not bothering to turn on a light, she crossed to the bed and sank onto its edge. She'd done it again—let down her guard and allowed Michael to affect her.

Her nose started to itch from holding back tears. How could she have been so blind, so stupid? She'd actually believed that she was over her feelings for him. She'd convinced herself that because she was eight years older she would also be wiser when it came to Michael. Katherine made a sound of self-disgust and flopped back against the mattress. Well, tonight her delusions about being indifferent and in control had been shattered—she was as susceptible to him at thirty as she'd been at eighteen. All it had taken was a couple of hours, a peanut-butter sandwich and the temptation of his mouth against hers.

Heat burned her cheeks as she thought of the way she'd parted her lips and clutched at his sweater. Could she have been any more obvious? Any more desperate?

Her eyes filled with tears, and she silently swore. The disappointment was even worse than the embarrassment. Without hope, there was nothing to lose, no chance for pain. And for an evening she'd indulged in a fantasy, then had let the fantasy blossom into hope.

Katherine dragged herself back into a sitting position. This was ridiculous. She was a grown woman, not a naive eighteen-year-old. Even if she couldn't conquer her feelings for Michael, she would suppress them. Sure she would.

Squaring her chin, Katherine stood, crossed to the bureau and opened the top drawer. Her flannel nightgown was there, and she pulled it out. The fabric's fuzzy texture was familiar, even comforting, against her palms, and she curled her fingers into it. Her mother had given her a gown like this every Christmas for as long as she could remember. This one was pink, white and perennially innocent; they were all practical—warm and sturdy and . . . anything but sexy.

The image of the gown from twelve years ago—white with a scattering of the tiniest blue flowers, as girlish and chaste as she herself had been—popped into her mind. It had been late February, and a night much like this one. She'd gone to bed early, having stayed up several nights running, studying for tests. At first the pounding had seemed to be a part of her dream. Then, gradually, she'd realized that the sound was coming from outside her head, and her eyes had drifted open.

"Katie, open up. Katie . . . I need you."

Michael. And soon as the realization had penetrated, she'd shot out of bed and across the room, not bothering to grab her glasses or robe. "What's wrong?" she'd asked, her voice quivering with a combination of concern and sleep. When he'd only groaned, she frantically went for the chain and lock, fumbling in her haste.

As soon as she opened the door, she knew he'd been drinking. He was leaning against the doorjamb, head lowered, coat unzipped. An admonition sprang to her lips.

Then he looked at her.

Katherine swallowed her lecture. Something was wrong. Something more than a few too many beers and too little sleep. Michael was hurting. Even without her glasses she could tell his dark eyes were wounded, his mouth etched with pain. She put a hand on his arm; the leather of his jacket was cold and brittle under her fingers. "Michael?"

The breath shuddered past his lips, and he slipped his arms around her, gathering her close. The winter night clung to him, but she didn't shiver or pull back. Instead, she pressed her cheek to his chest, trying to share her warmth, trying to comfort without words.

When the biting cold was replaced by searing warmth, he whispered, "I just needed to see you."

Even now, twelve years later, tears trickled from the corners of her eyes at the memory, and Katherine furiously swiped at them. That night was in the past; if she was to go on, it had to stay there.

Resolutely, she stood and undressed—slipping out of her sweatsuit, then socks; pulling her nightgown on. She shivered as the cool fabric slid over her warm skin. It was so frigid outside that even the carpeting under her bare feet was cold, and she went to the dresser for a fresh pair of sweat socks. Katherine took the carefully rolled socks out of the drawer, then stared down at them, her eyes misting over once again.

She'd done exactly the same thing twelve years ago. The night had been one of the coldest of the winter; the heating system in the old dormitory had been adequate at best. Michael used to tease her, claiming that the reason her feet were always cold was her blue blood—it was too thin. She'd pointed out that a socially prominent Chicago family and blue-blooded nobility were not the same thing. But in the end, her feet were still always cold...and wearing socks to bed had been part of her downfall.

Katherine made a sound that was a cross between a laugh and a groan as the memory unfolded in her head....

Michael had held her for a long time. She hadn't known what had happened or why he needed her, and it hadn't mattered. Michael had come to her. When his grip had become less urgent, less desperate, she'd slipped an arm around him and helped him to his room.

Between Michael's almost buckling weight and her being half-blind without her glasses, the lock almost proved an impossible feat. Almost, but not quite. The door swung open and Katherine grimaced as she squinted into the dark room—the floor was littered with all manner of things she couldn't quite make out. Swearing under her breath, she tightened her hold on

Michael and began to pick her way slowly toward his bed.

She did fine; it was Michael who was the problem. He refused to cooperate and it was like trying to navigate a one-hundred-and-eighty-pound sinking ship. "Dammit, Michael, only two more—"

Her foot landed on something that felt soft and squishy. Katherine squealed, tried to shift her weight too fast and lost her balance. As she tried to right herself, her sock-clad feet slid on the linoleum, and she and Michael tumbled to the bed, Michael landing on top.

Katherine's heart, already racing, tripled its beat. His body lay fully over hers, pressing her back into the soft mattress, his mouth so close that their breath met and mingled. In an attempt to steady herself, she sucked in air, then almost groaned aloud. He smelled of leather and sweat and faintly of beer. The combination was heady, male and Michael. Her hormones went crazy at the same moment she realized she was way out of her depth.

"Hi." Michael rested his forehead against hers, his lips curving, his voice husky.

"Hi," she returned, breathless, already aching.

He lifted his head so he could meet her eyes. "I'm sorry I woke you."

"It doesn't matter."

"Yeah, it does." He gently brushed the hair away from her face, then as if intrigued, he tangled his fingers in it. "It's the color of a midnight sky," he murmured, almost to himself. He rubbed the strands between his fingers. "And just as soft. Why haven't I ever noticed that before?"

Embarrassment washed over her, but she didn't lower her eyes, didn't try to move away. She couldn't. She'd waited forever for this moment. "You never looked," she whispered shyly.

"I'm looking now—" he trailed his fingers along her flushed cheekbones, then traced the arch of her dark eyebrows, the delicate curve of her chin and finally, the soft fullness of her lower lip "—you're beautiful, Katie."

As his eyes, hot and dark, dropped to her mouth, her head emptied of all rational thought and her mouth went dry. She dampened her suddenly parched lips with the tip of her tongue. His gaze followed the movement so intently that she squirmed beneath him. As she did, she felt his arousal. The blood rushed to her head, pleasure swamped her senses. Katherine flattened her hands on his chest but didn't apply an ounce of pressure. "I should go."

"Sweet, sweet Katie." He tightened his fingers in her hair. "Don't go."

Katherine drew in a shaky breath and stared helplessly up at him. She'd never been able to lie—not even to herself—and she'd never wanted anything more than to stay. She slid her hands up around his neck, tangling her fingers in the crisp, dark curls at his nape, silently acquiescing.

Michael released his breath in a long sigh. "My perfect Katie," he murmured, his lips curving, closing in. "What would I do without you?"

His mouth brushed hers, lightly, tentatively, cataclysmically. Katherine moaned and clutched at his jacket. She was lost. His words, his touch, were the stuff of her dreams. And at this moment her every dream was coming true. She could no more resist Michael than refuse oxygen, and she parted her lips and offered her tongue.

His kisses, which started out soft and sweet, became urgent, intoxicating. But she wasn't content to be led. She, totally inexperienced and untouched, went wild in his arms—demanding, offering, opening.

And he took what she offered, delving into her, his mouth muffling any sound she would have made at the quick stab of pain. With his arms cradling her as her body cradled him, they spiraled together to the heights, then plummeted back to earth.

When it was over, he brushed his hands over her damp cheeks, his eyes filled with regret, remorse, guilt. "Aw, Katie," he'd muttered, "I never meant—"

Katherine jerked herself back to the present and pressed the heels of her hands against her eyes. Remembering the look in his eyes and the apology that followed twisted in her gut like the worst case of flu. She'd been so humiliated, so hurt, she'd wanted to die. When she'd been sure he was asleep, she'd slipped quietly out of bed and gone back to her room.

The next day Michael had had a hangover. She'd known it the moment she'd seen him. She'd also known that he didn't remember anything of the night before. The truth of that had sliced her insides to shreds. It still did.

Katherine looked down at her hands, saw the moisture there, felt more of it on her cheeks and swore. It was time to move on. It was time to try—really try—to make a life for herself.

And Michael would never be a part of it—at least not the part she wanted him to be.

It was time she faced up to that fact. The truth was, up until now she'd only paid lip service to forgetting Michael, to moving on. Like a dieter who had willpower only until the dessert cart was rolled over, she had played games; deep down, she'd denied, hoped, made excuses.

No more. It was over.

Her feet were numb, and Katherine sat down and pulled on her socks. That done, she stood, turned back the blankets, then crawled underneath them. There were plenty of men who would be happy to take her out— good men who were handsome, bright, successful. Men like Dean Johnson.

Katherine pulled the covers up to her chin. Dean had been after her for months. He'd sent her flowers, called and cajoled. He was one of the most noted men in his branch of anthropology; he was as serious as she was. Why *not* say yes?

Ignoring the effort it took, she smiled. Tomorrow she would.

Tomorrow came too soon. As the first watery light of dawn appeared on the horizon, Katherine turned away from the window. She hadn't slept, not really. She'd tossed and turned and lain awake thinking about Michael and her vow of the night before. And the more she thought, the more she realized she wasn't sure she could do it.

Coffee would help, she decided staunchly. Reaching for her robe, she caught her reflection in the mirror. What did she need a robe for? Michael was never up before ten and besides—she ran a finger along the lace trim of her gown's high neck—it wasn't as if her full-length nightgown was at all sexy or revealing. She thought of silk, lace and sheerness...and simultaneously of Michael. His type of woman would choose effect over practicality. And you couldn't get much more practical than flannel. With a small grimace, she headed to the kitchen.

Light spilled from the open doorway. Thinking she'd left the light on, Katherine stepped into the room. She caught her breath as she saw she hadn't. Michael's back was to her as he stared into the refrigerator, and her gaze roamed slowly over him. He wasn't wearing a shirt. The olive skin tone of his Italian ancestors made him look slightly tanned even in the middle of February. His back was lean and muscled; there was a small white scar below his right shoulder blade. Idly wondering how he'd gotten it, she lowered her eyes. His jeans were loose, as if he'd recently lost weight, and dipped low on his hips. Her pulse fluttered as she realized he had nothing underneath that soft, faded denim.

She jerked her eyes away, counted to ten, then looked back at him. He was just a man, she reminded herself. That glorious expanse of muscled flesh was just a back. All men had backs, she had a back and—

And he'd changed in eight years, she thought, her heart rapping against her chest. He looked tougher, leaner. His contours seemed less round and more chiseled. She caught her bottom lip between her teeth. He was a man now instead of a boy.

As if he sensed her scrutiny, he straightened and looked over his shoulder at her. He didn't say a word, just stared at her in a fixed and unblinking way. He looked tired and tense, and she clasped her hands in front of her.

"You're up early," he finally said, his voice thick.

She glanced away, then back. "You, too."

"Yeah." He shut the refrigerator door, then leaned against it. "I guess I wasn't tired."

"Me, either." She shifted her weight from one foot to the other. "Not tired at all."

"I slept like a rock."

When he shoved his hands into his pockets, his jeans sloped even lower on his hips. It took all her self-control not to stare at the line of dark hair that disappeared under his waistband. "Oh . . . me, too."

"I'm glad," he murmured, his eyes dropping.

Katherine followed the direction of his gaze and blushed. "I should change."

Michael cleared his throat and tried to push away the image of soft pink-and-white fabric draped over womanly swells. "You're fine. I can't see . . . it's not like—" he coughed "—I mean, it's hardly transparent."

Katherine felt her blush deepen and cursed practical nightgowns and her own feelings of inadequacy. "Right. But still . . ." She began backing out of the doorway.

"Oh, sure." He shrugged, feigning disinterest. "If you'll feel more comforta—"

"I will, really." She turned and fled from the kitchen.

When she was gone Michael blew out a long, relieved breath and slumped against the refrigerator. For a moment he'd thought he was the one who would have to leave the room. That or turn his back on her. It had taken all his concentration to keep his eyes on her face. Even then, he hadn't been totally successful.

He dragged a hand through his hair and stared at the ceiling. God, she'd looked impossibly sexy in that concealing gown. All lacy and pink and pure. Like sugar and sunshine. He pictured her sweat socks peeking out from beneath the gown's hem and silently groaned. He would have been less affected if she'd had on a sheer teddy and nothing else.

He rubbed his forehead and realized he was sweating. There had to be a name for his illness, he thought with a shake of his head. He'd never read about anyone with a flannel fetish before. Boy, just admitting it made him feel like a pervert.

It had all started back in college. One morning he'd awakened with a huge hangover, a nonexistent memory and the most unbelievably erotic dream playing in his head. Starring in the dream had been himself, Katherine and a flannel nightgown. Even now, just thinking of it brought an ache of arousal and a picture that did nothing but intensify the ache.

He remembered waking up moaning her name, thinking she was with him. He'd looked around the room in confusion, then propped himself on an elbow and reached across the empty bed, only to find the sheets were cold.

A dream, he'd thought, falling back to the mattress, trying to piece together the previous evening. He'd gone to a party with his girlfriend. There she'd dropped him for a guy with a red Jag, but not before publicly throwing what he'd confided about his father back in his face. He'd set out to get mind-numbingly drunk. He remembered stumbling up the six flights of stairs to Katherine's dorm room, then pounding on her door. After that he'd drawn a complete blank—except for the impossible fantasy.

Michael shut his eyes again and the image that had haunted him for years, the image of him and Katherine in bed together, their lips clinging and parted, filled his head. He caught his breath as the reel played on the back of his eyelids, an arousal as intense as the one that morning twelve years ago tightening in his belly. He could almost feel her flannel gown brush against his flesh, soft and inviting. And under the fabric, her warm, silky skin.

In his head, they rolled together, a tangle of arms and legs and sheets. Then she was beneath him, urging him with her hands and hips, and he slipped inside her. She was warm and tight and felt as if she were made for him. His mouth caught her cry of pleasure and they rocked—

"Michael, are you all right?"

Michael's head snapped up at the sound of Katherine's voice. She stood in the doorway, wearing the gray sweatsuit from the night before. "Fine," he choked out, spinning around to face the counter. He breathed deeply through his nose and prayed she hadn't looked at the front of his jeans. "I was just ... getting ready to make coffee."

"Good. I could really use a..." Her words trailed off. His back was stiff and he hadn't made a move toward the coffeepot. She took an uncertain step into the kitchen. "Are you sure you're all right? You looked, well, like you were in pain."

He was in pain all right—painfully aroused. "I was just thinking," he answered shortly, then almost laughed out loud. Wouldn't she be shocked if she knew what he'd been thinking? He reached for the coffeepot. His hands shook slightly, and he cursed his imagination and all manufacturers of flannel everywhere.

His curt tone was like a slap in the face, and Katherine squared her shoulders. He didn't want to talk—that was fine with her. It would make it that much easier to distance herself from him. Besides, he'd no doubt been thinking about some woman who owned a closet full of sheer black nighties.

She folded her arms across her chest. "I just wanted to remind you that our first interview is today at ten-thirty."

"I haven't forgotten." Michael kept his eyes trained on the coffee dripping into the pot. "We might as well go together."

Katherine bit back a tart reply and tilted her chin up. "Fine," she said coolly. "I'll meet you at the front door at ten-fifteen."

Marilyn and Ron Fuss looked like scientists, Michael decided as he and Katherine stepped into the office where their interview would be conducted. Ron had nondescript brown hair that was thinning and slightly frizzy, Marilyn's was bright red and cut in a short boyish style. Both wore wire-rimmed glasses and serious expressions.

Michael shifted his gaze from the two behind the desk to Katherine. She seemed calm and absolutely at ease. He scowled. His own heart felt like a sledgehammer in his chest, which was ridiculous. This interview was no big deal...and last night had been just one of those things. A fluke. He was a man, she was a woman, one thing had led to... He scowled again as a knot of desire tightened in his abdomen.

"Hi, Dr. Reed, Michael." Ron came around the desk, hand outstretched. "I'm going to leave you in Marilyn's capable hands. Roger and Jean are waiting for me next door."

After they'd murmured the appropriate greetings and Ron had left the room, they took a seat. Marilyn smiled. "How are you?"

Katherine folded her hands in her lap to hide their trembling. How was she going to handle this interview? She had only two choices—reveal herself to Michael or act unprofessionally by lying to Marilyn—and both made her stomach churn. "Fine," she finally answered, her voice sounding shaky to her own ears.

"How about you, Michael?" the woman asked.

Michael slouched in his chair, thought of his sleepless night and the reason for it, and promptly lied. "No problems here."

"Good." Marilyn smiled again. "Did you two see much of each other this week?"

"Not really," Katherine answered quickly. Too quickly, she realized, and silently swore.

"Yeah," Michael repeated, an image of Katie bending and stretching filling his head. He pushed the image away. "Hardly at all."

Marilyn jotted something on the paper in front of her. "Could you be more specific?"

Katherine felt her cheeks warm and hoped Marilyn didn't notice their color. She crossed her legs. "Once. Last night."

"Twice," Michael corrected, shifting in his seat. "If you count this morning."

"Mmm-hmm." Marilyn slid her glasses back up to the bridge of her nose. "How about food?"

"Food?" Katherine echoed, realizing in dismay that her palms were damp.

"Yes. Did you share a meal together?"

"No."

"Yes."

They answered oppositely in unison, and Katherine cleared her throat. "I wasn't counting peanut-butter sandwiches and...um—" She remembered in perfect sensory detail Michael handing her her plate, remembered the way his fingers had brushed hers and the shock that had gone through her at the accidental touch. She cleared her throat again. ''—and corn chips.''

''I see.'' Marilyn jotted down another note. ''Mr. Tardo...Michael, have you noticed any changes?''

Michael jerked his gaze from the small window behind the desk back to Marilyn Fuss. He blinked, confused. He'd been picturing a time when he'd been in a lot of pain and Katie had held and comforted him. But the strange part was, it was an event he couldn't remember ever having occurred. ''I'm sorry,'' he repeated. ''What?''

''Have you noticed any changes in your daily routine—eating, sleeping, recreational patterns?''

Michael tried to shelve the memory but it continued to pluck at him. Distracted, he shook his head. ''Nope, none.''

''Dr. Reed? How about you?''

Katherine opened her mouth to answer, then shut it. She darted a quick, furtive glance at Michael. No, he hadn't had any trouble sleeping, she thought, suddenly angry. Nor was he the one who'd been maneuvered into an uncomfortable position. In eight years nothing had changed.

''Dr. Reed?''

''I'm sorry,'' Katherine said tightly, feeling like a hypocrite, ''no changes.''

''You're both sure? Think carefully, something that might seem insignificant to you could be exactly what we're looking for. You'd be surprised how often minor behavior changes become predictable patterns.'' Marilyn's brow wrinkled as she scanned the paper in front of her. ''Michael? Anything?''

Michael folded his arms across his chest, thinking again of the previous evening. "Sorry, I can't help you out."

"Dr. Reed?"

Katherine had difficulty meeting her student's eyes. "Maybe next time."

"Well, that was easy," Marilyn said, tossing down her pencil and grinning. "If neither of you have any questions, you're finished. See you next week."

Katherine swallowed past the lump in her throat and stood. "Thanks, Marilyn. You did fine."

"You really think so?" Marilyn brightened. "I was more tense about interviewing you than any of the others. I hope you weren't offended that I asked you about changes twice. I know that you, of all people, know how import—"

"Don't give it a second thought," Katherine interrupted, wanting to crawl under the desk. "You were the picture of professionalism." It was true—the student had been more professional than the teacher. All Katherine could think about was getting away from Marilyn's trusting expression, and she started to edge toward the door. "I'll see you in class on Monday."

With a final wan smile, Katherine slipped out of the office and into the frigid hallway. It seemed twice as cold after the closeness of the office, and she shivered and pulled on her coat.

"It's like a tomb in here," Michael muttered, irritated. He yanked up his jacket zipper.

"You can say that again." Not looking at him, Katherine made a beeline for the double glass doors at the end of the hall.

"Hey." Michael grabbed her elbow to slow her down. "Where's the fire?"

"Let go of my arm," she said through clenched teeth.

"Pardon me." Michael dropped his hand. "I thought it was boring, too, but at least I can be civil."

"It?" she repeated, glaring at him, spoiling for a fight. "Surely you don't mean the interview?"

"Surely I do," Michael said, just as frustrated, just as ready to argue. "Any ideas what we should do for an encore? Go to the mall and watch the shoppers? Or maybe to a drive-in and take notes of what people eat? We could spend the whole day keeping tab on who orders cheeseburgers versus plain, diet soda versus sugared. Now *that* would be scientifically significant."

Her face burning, Katherine turned on him. "You have no idea how important this experiment is! But then your highest priority has always been having a good time." She pushed through the glass doors at the end of the hall and stepped outside.

She sounded prim and self-righteous, and he was reminded of an eighteen-year-old boy, out of control and running as fast as he could. And until a week ago he'd thought he'd put away that part of his past. Now he thought about little else, and the memories ate at him.

As soon as he'd cleared the doors, he lashed out at her. "Do I hear one of your famous lectures coming on?"

She didn't look at him. "Which lecture are you referring to? The one about taking responsibility for your life or the one about acting like an adult?"

Michael had parked in an illegal spot right in front of the building. He plucked the ticket from the windshield, stuffed it in his pocket, then turned to glare at her. "I'm sure either of those would do," he said tightly. "Do you remember how they go, or should I start one for you?"

She flexed her fingers. "Start one? Does that mean you actually listened to me? Surprise, surprise."

Michael unlocked the car and yanked open her door. Without waiting for her to get in, he went around to the other side. He slid behind the wheel, started the car, then backed out of the parking space so fast the tires squealed. When they'd pulled into traffic moments later, he looked at her. "Did you ever give me a choice?"

She narrowed her eyes at his tone. "What's that supposed to mean?"

"You're the one with the Ph.D. Figure it out." He gunned the engine to pass a delivery truck.

She tipped up her chin. "If you have something to say, Michael, say it."

He tightened his grip on the steering wheel. "I see you haven't changed. Still the conscientious little browbeater." He accelerated and slid through a yellow light.

The last threads of her control snapped and she whirled on him, all the frustration, anger and vulnerability she'd felt since the study began bubbling to the surface. "At least I try."

"Mind deciphering that, Professor?"

Katherine gripped the dashboard as he took a corner too fast. "Well, you haven't strayed far from wine, women and song, have you?"

Michael muttered a short, blunt word. She thought he was the same irresponsible boy he'd been eight years ago. The only difference was, then she'd believed in him. That she didn't anymore was like a fist to his chest. "What's wrong, Princess?" Michael roared into her driveway and screeched to a halt. "The profession of barkeeper not good enough for you?"

Princess! She wanted to throttle him. "Why are you so sensitive? Guilty conscience?"

"And when did you become your parents?"

Katherine's breath caught at the comment. Her parents were critical of everyone and everything outside their social and economic sphere. Michael knew how much she hated their elitism, but he had thrown them in her face anyway. Shooting him a furious glance, she grabbed the door handle and tumbled from the car.

Michael was out and around to her side before she'd even managed to regain her footing. He pinned her between himself and the door. "Oh no, we're going to finish this."

There was nowhere to look but his eyes; the expression in them was murderous. Katherine lifted her chin and glared at him. "Finish what? Name-calling? Repeating history?" As soon as she said the last, she regretted it. How many times had she wished she could repeat history to change it? And here she was, eight years later, repeating history and making all the same mistakes. "Let me go," she said fiercely, feeling tears welling behind her eyes but vowing not to cry.

Michael stared down at her, his jaw clenched so tightly it hurt. Her lips were full and slightly parted; he knew she would taste sweet, like overripe strawberries. His gut tightened as the need to take her mouth raced over him.

He dropped his hands to her shoulders and gave in to the need. He caught her mouth, not gently, not tentatively, but with force born of need too long denied. Her lips were cold, but only at first. They warmed, then parted. Her small sound of surprise became a strangled sigh; her hands flattened against his chest, then clutched at his lapels. He hadn't known how she would react, hadn't paused to worry. He'd only known that he wanted to kiss her—had wanted to for what seemed like forever.

Michael moved his hands lower, using the leverage to press her more fully to him. Maybe he'd wanted to taste her mouth since that morning twelve years ago when he'd awakened alone and aching for her. And twelve years was a long time to wait. Too long. The need ripped through him, and he deepened the kiss.

Katherine didn't question, didn't think of resisting or refusing. Instead, she sagged against him, offering him her tongue, taking his. He tasted of passion and fury and something else. Something dangerous that swamped her senses and made her forget yesterdays and tomorrows—made her forget everything but his lips against hers.

With a shudder, she slid her hands up to his shoulders and held on. Michael was taking her to a place she'd never been before—not in her most potent dreams, nor even her most cherished memory. The place was sweet, dark, mindless. She gave herself over to it, and to him. She only asked that she never have to leave.

Without breaking the kiss, Michael turned them around so that his back was against the car. He leaned against the cold metal and took her full weight, slight as she was. He needed the car's support because he was shaken to the core. Tiny, fragile, five-foot-nothing Katie packed the punch of a heavyweight champ—he'd been leveled with the first touch of her lips to his. He wondered if he would ever be steady again.

He yanked at the satin ribbon at her nape and her hair tumbled about them, a shiny, black cape. He wrapped his fingers in the thick, dark mass and the herbal scent of her shampoo tickled his nose. Dragging his mouth from hers, he found the sensitive curve of her ear, then the place where her pulse beat wildly in her throat. His progress was stopped by a barrier of wool, and he groaned. They were wearing too many clothes.

Even as he reached for the first of the offending coat buttons, his eyes snapped open. They were outdoors, it was February and freezing, someone could see them...and none of that mattered. He wanted Katie underneath him and naked; he wanted to feel her smooth flesh against his, wanted to hear her pleasure as he slipped into her.

He wound his fingers possessively in her hair as the words she'd flung at him filled his head. *Was* he repeating history? If he was, it was a history more distant than his and Katie's—more distant and much more painful. He looked down at her and worked to control his ragged breathing. And if history was to be repeated, wouldn't that make him no better than the father who'd begun it?

Michael dropped his hands and set her away from him. Her eyes opened, at first confused, then hurt. The look twisted his gut. But the truth was, he was the type of guy who would make a life out of hurting her.

Katherine realized she was still clutching his jacket at the same instant she became aware that he wasn't touching her at all. Color stung her cheeks, and she jerked herself upright.

"You were right, Katie," he said softly, trailing a finger along her jaw. Her skin was as soft as down and he lingered over it as a convicted felon would linger over his last moment of freedom. Finally, regretfully, he lowered his hand. "Repeating history isn't such a great idea."

Without another word, he turned on his heel, went around the car and climbed in. Katherine watched him until the restored Corvette disappeared into the snarl of cars on North Main. Letting out her breath in a single shaky sigh, she went inside.

Five

The following Saturday morning Katherine unlocked her office door and turned on the light. For today's interview she and Michael were being seen separately, and, luckily, she'd drawn Marilyn. Knowing her student would be there any moment, she slipped hurriedly out of her coat and gloves. She needed every extra minute to prepare herself for what she had to say.

Katherine looked down at her trembling hands. She was withdrawing from the study. It had been inevitable from the first, but she'd tried to fool herself—into believing she was immune to Michael, into thinking she could be objective.

She sank into the chair behind her desk, then dropped her head into her hands. Objective? That was a laugh. Twelve years ago she'd taken one look at Michael Tardo and objectivety had been lost forever. She'd recognized the truth of that at eighteen, why hadn't she been able to at thirty? She sighed. It seemed that pride, age and stupidity grew in direct proportion to one another.

She swiveled around in her chair to look out the one small window her office boasted. The past week had been her idea of hell. Michael had surprised her by being around quite a lot, but he'd been short with her to the point of gruffness. That was, when he had bothered to acknowledge her presence at all.

It was what she'd originally wanted—not to go back to the friends they had been or forward to some new relationship, but to cautiously avoid each other. But what she'd wanted and what she felt were two very different things. And it was tearing her apart.

"Morning, Prof. You okay?"

Katherine peered over her shoulder at Marilyn. "And to think I doubted you had the intuitive skills required of the social scientist."

"Sarcasm? My, my, you *are* in bad shape. Would a breakfast of overprocessed white flour, sugar, preservatives and a dozen other ingredients whose names I can't pronounce help?" Marilyn waved a bag from a well-known doughnut chain.

Katherine smiled for the first time that morning. "You eat entirely too much junk."

"Yeah, so what else is new?"

Shaking her head, Katherine swiveled back around and motioned her student to come in. Marilyn Fuss was brilliant but eccentric. She'd attended Rock River College as an undergraduate, had earned her degree, gotten married, then both she and her husband had come back to complete their educations. Not only was she one of Katherine's best students, but over the years they'd transcended the student-teacher relationship to become friends.

Marilyn dropped the bag on the desk, then pulled a thermos out of her tote. "Hangover?" When Katherine only arched an eyebrow, Marilyn laughed and poured two cups of coffee. "Okay, so what's up?"

Katherine selected a sugar-sprinkled jelly doughnut, then passed the bag back. "Marilyn, how old are you?"

"Twenty-eight." Marilyn picked out a doughnut caked with powdered sugar and grinned. "I buy most of my clothes secondhand and dye my hair. But then, I'm supposed to be interviewing you."

"True." Katherine nudged her untouched pastry. She didn't want to do this; she had no choice. If she didn't she wouldn't be able to live with herself. "Have you ever totally embarrassed yourself in front of me?"

This time, Marilyn's eyebrows arched. "Although that does sound like my style, I'm curious. Why do you want to know?"

"I was hoping you had because—" Katherine cleared her throat "—I'm about to do the same."

Marilyn shook her head in disbelief. "Not the cool, collected Dr. Katherine Reed? Not the professor who—"

"I'm withdrawing from the experiment."

"What!"

"I have to." Katherine couldn't meet the other woman's eyes so she pushed away from the desk and stood. She crossed to the bookshelves. Needing something to do with her hands, she trailed a finger along the dusty volumes. "All last week I was torn... between embarrassment and professionalism. Between the need to hide and the need to do my job." She brushed the dust from her fingers, then turned back to Marilyn. "In a minute I'm going to feel even more ridiculous than I do now."

"This is about Michael."

It wasn't a question, and Katherine colored. She wanted to deny it; she wanted to go on pretending. She faced Marilyn instead. "Michael and I have a past relationship."

"You were friends. He told me, and I—"

"We were more than friends...we were lovers." Her hands were trembling again. Katherine slipped them into her pockets and proceeded to sketch out the details for Marilyn.

When she'd finished, Marilyn let out a long, low whistle. "Why didn't you say something?"

"I felt trapped. Michael had already cleared our being friends with you and Ron and was pressing me for an answer. He wanted to know why I was so opposed to his participation." She pulled her hands out of her pockets and gestured nervously. "I thought I could handle it. I thought I was past any feelings I had for him. I thought—"

"You're in love with him," Marilyn said in a no-nonsense tone of voice.

Katherine groaned. "I shouldn't have joked about your intuitive powers."

"What do you plan to do?" Marilyn pushed her doughnut aside and rested her elbows on the desk.

"Withdraw from the study." Katherine sat back down. "There's no other way. From the first my participation weakened it."

"Not that." Marilyn shot her an exasperated look. "What do you plan to do about your feelings for Michael? After all, you can't catch him if you don't chase him."

Katherine shook her head. "I did enough chasing to last a lifetime. Besides, right now the only thing I should be concerned with is the study and its success."

Marilyn made a clucking noise with her tongue as she tapped her index finger against her bottom lip. "How does he feel about you?"

"He has no romantic interest in me; he never will. He thinks of himself as a friend and big brother."

"But—"

"Give it up, Marilyn," Katherine warned, reaching for her coffee.

Marilyn plucked at her bright red bob. "Have you considered what Michael's going to say when you tell him you've withdrawn from the study? Or how you're going to explain this to the other students?"

Katherine's hand paused halfway to her lips. She hadn't. She'd been so intent on facing Marilyn this morning, she hadn't considered facing Michael or the other students later. How could she explain? Every option she came up with was more mortifying than the last.

"I can see by your expression that you haven't." Marilyn leaned back in her chair. "I have a proposal to make. One that gets you off the hot seat—with Michael and the study." At Katherine's interested glance, she went on. "You continue as if nothing has changed. You live with Michael, you meet with me for the weekly interviews. Say whatever you want because I won't include it in the statistics."

"What about Michael?"

"What about him?" Marilyn lifted her hands, palms up. "You already said he doesn't think of you as anything more than a friend...that he never will. I see no reason why we can't continue to monitor his behavior.

In fact, why don't we tell him from now on the interviews will all be conducted separately. That way he'll feel free from the constraints of your past relationship to answer honestly. And you won't even have to show.''

"It's the perfect out for me," Katherine murmured, meeting Marilyn's eyes gratefully. "No wonder you're my prize student."

Marilyn grinned. "And I was my mamma's prize baby."

Katherine returned her smile. "Yeah, but I bet she hates that hair."

Marilyn patted her spiky red hairdo and stood. "Now that that's settled, I'm going to meet my honey to correlate this week's responses. We have some interesting situations developing."

"Oh?"

"Mmm-hmm." She slung her book bag and coat over her arm. "Sid and Janet hate each other. They've used textbooks to section off areas of the apartment as 'hers' and 'his.' On another front, Mary's gorilla boyfriend threatened to rearrange Tim's face and now Tim's afraid to even talk to her."

Katherine bit back a smile. "It's pretty hard to watch for subtle behavioral changes with the threat of death hanging over your head."

"Tell me about it." Marilyn stopped at the door. "Here's my personal favorite. Sweet, shy Tracy Lynn has decided Nick is sexier than, get this, 'Mick Jagger and Bruce Willis' and is acting like a groupie. Nick thinks it's disgusting and has made noises about quitting."

Katherine couldn't help herself and threw her head back and laughed. "I'm sorry, it's just that I can't imagine Tracy—''

"I know," Marilyn said miserably, hitching her book bag onto her shoulder. "So far, no one's responding as anticipated."

Katherine heard the disappointment in her student's voice and her smile faded. She knew how frustrating research could be. Her little bomb this morning hadn't helped. "Chin up. This is only the second week. And remember, the two things that are most important here are the information gained through the research, whether it proves or disproves your hypothesis, and adhering to a scholarly, scientific approach. Besides, you'll be surprised by what develops in the next couple of weeks."

Marilyn brightened visibly and shot Katherine a mischievous grin. "I'm already surprised." Hand on the doorknob, she looked back over her shoulder. "Teach?"

"Hmm?" Katherine glanced back up at Marilyn.

"I still say, you can't catch something you refuse to chase." With that, she ducked out of the office.

Katherine frowned at the now empty doorway, Marilyn's words running through her head. *You can't catch something you refuse to chase.* That doesn't apply here, Katherine told herself, drumming her fingers against the open book in front of her. She'd given it her best shot. Sure she had. In college she'd . . .

Katherine drew her eyebrows together, stilling her fingers. In college she'd what? Hidden her feelings behind a mask of a friend and waited and hoped and prayed that suddenly he would see her as more than one.

She shifted uncomfortably in her seat. And if she was facing facts, she might as well face them all. The fact was, she'd never once let Michael know what she wanted or what she felt. She'd never been honest with him ... or herself. How could she? She'd been too busy denying and hiding.

Chasing Michael? she thought again, the corners of her mouth lifting in a mocking smile. She'd been running in the opposite direction.

There was a strange trembling in the pit of her stomach; Katherine pushed the sensation away. It didn't matter what she'd done. Even without her Coke-bottle glasses she wasn't Michael's type. She'd seen the women he dated. They were beautiful and vivacious and ...

And she was a defeatist, Katherine realized, the trembling sensation spreading. A defeatist and a coward. She'd always thought of herself as decisive. She'd always taken pride in the fact that she knew what she wanted and went after it. She always knew what she wanted all right—but she didn't always go after it. Not in her personal life. Not when she had something that could be wounded—like her heart or pride.

Katherine looked down at her hands; they were shaking. All this time she'd loved Michael but had never given them a chance. She'd been too much of a coward.

Katherine stiffened her spine. Ridiculous, that's what it was! She was a grown woman, independent and intelligent. She should go after what she wanted!

The niggling doubt still remained, manifesting itself as an image of what every woman she'd ever known Michael to date looked like. She pictured long, flowing hair, a lush, long-legged figure and flashy clothes.

Katherine scowled and pulled a compact out of her top desk drawer. She peered into the tiny mirror, turning this way and that, appraising herself. She was attractive, not flashy, not knockout beautiful, but attractive

Katherine snapped the compact shut and tossed it back into the drawer. This wasn't about looks; it was about attitude. Could she be Michael's *type* of woman?

Katherine caught her bottom lip between her teeth. One couldn't acquire attitude over the counter. One couldn't buy a husky laugh and come-hither smile in a department store. Michael's women liked to laugh instead of analyze, liked to flirt and tease and take chances. Could she do it?

Anger at her own cowardice had the blood rushing to her cheeks. She was always whining about repeating history. Now was her chance to change it. She wanted Michael and she would do everything in her power to make him want her. Starting now, she was taking charge of her life.

Grabbing her purse, she took the first step.

Seven hours later, Katherine pirouetted in front of her bedroom mirror. She'd been in front of the glass fifteen minutes; she still couldn't believe the transformation. The hairdresser had snipped and shaped and molded. The style was more flirtatious than sexy. With a delighted smile, she shook her head, enjoying the way the long layers swung with the movement. She lowered her eyes. A helpful saleswoman had suggested soft, feminine clothes, convincing her she was too tiny to carry off the high-fashion look she'd been sure she wanted.

The woman was good at her job, Katherine thought, pleasure warming her cheeks. The sweater was angora, pure white with a scooped neckline and long, fitted sleeves. The black-and-white herringbone skirt was short and artfully coy, with attached pleats that skimmed over her hips, flaring at midthigh. As she moved, the fabric played peekaboo with her knees.

Katherine smoothed the sweater over her hips, and as she thought of the wispy bits of lace underneath, her cheeks went from pink to rose. She felt absolutely wicked.

Now for the test—facing Michael. She needed to be fun, flirtatious; she needed to let him know what she wanted. He was at the bar; he'd left a note that he was shorthanded and would be working tonight. Katherine drew a deep breath. Maybe a public launch would be better than a private one, anyway—a drink couldn't hurt. Letting out her breath in a determined hiss, she decided this was it.

The bar was slow for a Saturday night. Michael glanced around the nearly empty room and hoped the students had exams, a prom or some other event scheduled for tonight. If they didn't, he could be in trouble. He shot a smile at the bored waitress and thought fleetingly about letting her go home, then rejected the thought. The bar business was as unpredictable as the people who frequented them—at eight the place could be dead, by nine, packed.

He frowned. Tonight, being a single bartender serving a capacity crowd could be a blessing—he wouldn't have time to think about Katie. His frown deepened, and he wished someone would order a drink. When no one did, he admitted the truth—she was all he'd been able to think about. Katie in his arms: warm, passionate, totally his. Katie's lips parting, her hands clutching. Katie wearing a flannel gown and sweat socks...her feet sliding on the linoleum...the two of them falling to the bed.

Michael shook his head. He had better get a grip on his over-sexed imagination—now he was inventing things that had never happened.

Michael looked at his watch, cursed under his breath, then checked the clock behind the bar. Before he'd lost his head and let his hormones take over, he and Katherine had been getting along so well. He'd had Katie back in his life. It'd been like old times and . . .

Michael grimaced. What a laugh. What he'd felt since the moment he'd stepped into her apartment had nothing to do with the platonic friendship they'd shared in college, and everything to do with being a man . . . a man living with a beautiful woman.

He plucked a cocktail straw from the box and tapped it against the bar. Dammit, where had this need, this gnawing want, come from? He ached for her in a way he would have thought impossible. He certainly hadn't asked for it. All he'd ever expected from her was friendship. He didn't want to complicate things; he didn't want a relationship and all the hurt feelings that came with its inevitable end. Because he knew it *would* come to an end.

Disgusted, he tossed the straw in the trash. Katherine wasn't a woman to be trifled with. She wasn't a woman who would casually start an affair or just as casually end it. She needed commitments, promises. She didn't have to tell him that—he just knew.

And he could never give her either.

He glanced up as he felt the trickle of cold air from the door. At first he thought he was mistaken; it couldn't be Katie. But it was. She looked his way and smiled, and his heart slammed into his throat. What was she doing here?

She hung her coat on one of the antique brass hooks by the door and headed toward him, a subtle swing to her walk, her mouth curving once again into a smile.

Michael swallowed hard. She looked different. Sexy. He realized he was staring at the place where fuzzy white fabric ended and smooth white flesh began and jerked his gaze back to hers.

Katherine put her hands on the bar rail and leaned toward him. "Hello, Michael." Her voice was husky, a little breathless.

Michael struggled to keep his eyes on her face. He was only partially successful. "Hi." The word sounded choked; he scowled and tried again. "This is a surprise."

She looked down, then back up at him through a sweep of thick, dark lashes. "A good one, I hope."

Michael noticed two guys at the end of the bar looking her way. "Sure, of course. I'm always happy to see a—" from the corner of his eyes, he saw the guys pick up their drinks and start down the bar "—a...um, friend. Have a seat."

She turned her head to glance around the bar, then slid onto a stool. "I wouldn't want to disturb you while you're working."

He furiously wiped the bar top in front of her with a damp rag. "You're not disturbing me." She was driving him crazy instead. And he was acting like a seventeen-year-old virgin. He tried to pull himself together. "You cut your hair." His voice was thick, almost gruff, and he nearly groaned out loud. So much for another tack.

Katherine ran a hand through the layers. "Just a little. Do you like it?"

"God, yes." Her silky black hair slid over and between her fingers. He imagined his own hands threading through the midnight strands. Michael jerked his gaze away. "The usual?"

"Uh-uh." She tipped her head back, her smile brilliant. "I think I want something—I don't know, more exciting."

"Exciting?"

"Mmm..." She lightly touched her index finger to her lips, then caught it between her teeth. "I know, I'll have a martini."

"A martini?" Feeling a little unsteady, Michael drew a deep breath. It didn't help, and he silently swore.

"A gin martini. Very dry, shaken not stirred."

"James Bond's drink?" Michael asked, raising his eyebrows.

She lowered her lashes. "I said I wanted exciting."

"Right," he muttered, gritting his teeth as the guys from down the bar reseated themselves a stool away from Katherine. She seemed oblivious to both their move and interest. As he made her drink, he kept his eyes on them all, knowing he was acting like a protective lover but unable to stop.

A carryover from their college days, Michael reassured himself, skewering an olive and dropping it into the glass. He was watching out for her, that's all. As he set the drink in front of her, he shot the two men a narrow-eyed glance.

"Thanks." Katherine trailed a finger around the rim of the glass, then dipped it into the cold, wet liquid. She brought the finger to her mouth.

Michael's eyes followed the movement, a lump forming in his throat. Resisting the urge to take her drink away and send her back home, he murmured, "So, what brings you out tonight?"

She lifted the glass to her lips. "I wanted to have some fun."

"Fun?"

"Mmm, fun." She sipped the potent liquid, her eyes never leaving his. "Any suggestions?"

He had a suggestion all right—and so did every other man within twenty feet. He loosened his suddenly snug collar. "Lower you voice, Katie."

"Lower? Why?" She leaned forward, her eyes earnest. As she did, the neckline of her sweater slipped, revealing the top of a creamy, round breast—softer, whiter than the sweater.

Michael's mouth went dry; his temperature skyrocketed. He turned away on the pretense of pouring himself a soda. While he filled the glass, he breathed deeply through his nose and told himself that he absolutely was not jealous. So what if every guy in the place was wishing, praying and hoping for a chance with her? So what if she wasn't wearing a bra? It wasn't any concern of his.

He swung back around and saw red. One of the slimeballs to her right had started a conversation—and it looked to Michael like the guy was conversing with her chest. The urge to grab the man by the neck and throw him out of the bar surged through him.

He shoved his hands into his pockets, checking the urge, feeling shaken. This had to stop. He had no interest in Katie other than—He watched as she took another sip of her drink, watched as her neck arched slightly, saw her tongue dart out to catch a drop of moisture on her full bottom lip. His chest tightened. He was in serious trouble.

With more force than necessary, but as lightly as he could manage, he set his soda on the bar in front of her. "Excuse me, I need to see to my other customers."

Forty minutes later, Katherine glanced at Michael from under lowered lashes, a sinking sensation in her stomach. Michael was at the other end of the bar, talking to the waitress. She pursed her lips. In the last forty minutes he'd talked to everyone in the bar—everyone, that was, except her.

She looked down at her empty glass. It wasn't working. She'd tried. She'd talked, flirted and teased; the more she had, the quieter, the more preoccupied he'd become. From the first, he'd seemed angry and uncomfortable.

Katherine caught herself shredding her cocktail napkin and dropped her hands to her lap. In a last-ditch effort to get a reaction out of him, she'd talked with the guys sitting next to her. Nothing! At least they'd been attentive! Michael couldn't even be bothered to get her another dr—

"Katherine, what a pleasure!"

She swung around. Dean Johnson had come up behind her. It looked as if he was alone. She smiled with relief. At least she would have someone to talk to now. "Dean! What are you doing here?"

He slid onto the stool next to her. "I'm going up to the college to hear Norman French's lecture. I thought I'd stop by for a drink first." He knocked on the bar to get Michael's attention. "Are you alone?"

Katherine felt color creep up her cheeks, and told herself that it was perfectly acceptable for a thirty-year-old woman to be sitting alone in a bar on a Saturday night. She felt as if she'd been caught red-handed anyway. She cleared her throat. "Yes, I didn't have any plans tonight so—"

"Great." Dean tapped on the bar again. "Why don't you come with me? It promises to be an excellent lecture. French is the most noted man in his field."

"Oh, I don't know..." She saw Michael coming their way and used the interruption to stall Dean. The truth was, even though Michael was ignoring her, she didn't want to give up yet. When he stopped in front of them, she made the introductions. "Michael, I'd like you to meet Dean Johnson. He's an anthropology professor at the—"

"We've met before," Michael said shortly, staring at the other man, making no effort to hide the fact he was sizing him up. From his neatly trimmed beard to his tweed jacket, Dean Johnson was pure professor and just the type of man Katherine preferred. Michael narrowed his eyes. This was also the "yes" man who'd sent her flowers, the same man he'd seen here in the bar hitting on the coeds. If this overeducated skirt-chaser laid one finger on Katie, he would throttle him. "I never forget a customer," he added meaningfully, holding out his hand. "Michael Tardo... Katie's roommate."

The other man hesitated, then recognition flashed in his eyes, and he took Michael's hand. "Katherine's study partner."

Michael gave the man a slow, satisfied smile. "I suppose you could call it that."

Katherine's breath caught. What was he doing? Michael made it sound as though... Dean would think that they were... She stiffened. She knew exactly what he was up to—he was playing big brother. The few guys she'd dated in college had been bullied, intimidated and finally, sent packing by Michael. Back then, she'd fantasized all sorts of romantic reasons why he didn't want her with another man; now she had enough experience and objectivity to know he imagined himself some modern-day knight in shining armor and her an innocent damsel in distress.

Whatever his intentions, it was embarrassing. Dean was a colleague; she had a reputation to protect. Katherine lifted her chin. "Dean was just telling me about a lecture tonight at the college."

"Oh?" Michael folded his arms across his chest.

"Indeed," Dean inserted. "I was trying to convince Katherine to go with me. Norman French is speaking on pre-Colombian pottery. It's tonight only and sure to be gripping."

"I'm sure." Michael's mouth curved in amusement. "And what did she say?"

That he could so blithely ask the question made her blood boil. She would show Michael Tardo! With a brilliant smile, she turned to Dean. "I was about to say, I'd love to go."

"Great." Dean rubbed his hands together. "I think we still have time for that drink. Michael, bring me a glass of white wine...and get Katherine another."

Without another word, Michael took her empty glass and moved down the bar to get their drinks. Katherine watched him for a moment, then dropped her eyes to the bar. Michael didn't care at all that another man had just asked her out and that she'd accepted! He hadn't even looked at her! She'd gone to all this trouble, and he wasn't affected at all.

Well, she wasn't about to sit around feeling miserable. Katherine tossed her head. She'd given it a chance; it hadn't worked. Who cared? *She* certainly didn't. She and Dean were going to have a lovely time. It might even be the start of—

"Here you are." Michael set the drinks in front of them and some of Dean's wine sloshed over the side and onto the cocktail napkin. Michael replaced the napkin, his full attention on the other man. "I've always been fascinated by pre-Columbian pottery," he murmured. "But I haven't been able to find a definitive text on the subject. What do you suggest?"

Without any further prompting, Dean launched into a description of several. While he orated on the subject, Katherine picked up her drink, annoyed. Michael was trying to make Dean look like a pretentious jerk. Well, it wouldn't work. So what if Dean had found a way to mention both his graduate days at Columbia and the number of articles he'd had published while discussing a totally unrelated subject? So what if he had gotten so carried away he'd forgotten she was there? She *was* going to enjoy this evening.

Katherine lifted the glass to her lips and sipped. Her eyes widened in surprise, then flew to Michael's. When he cocked his head and grinned at her, her blood pressure skyrocketed. The drink was nothing but water with an olive tossed in for effect! This was going too far! She would not let him decide how much she could or could not drink and opened her mouth to tell him so, then shut it again as she realized how the whole scenario would look to Dean.

Katherine met Michael's amused gaze with her own furious one. She drained the glass and pushed it across the bar toward him. He smiled and shook his head, and she narrowed her eyes. Of all the arrogant, infuriating, interfering... She cleared her throat. "Excuse me, Dean. Won't the lecture be starting soon?"

"Right you are." Dean pulled out his wallet. "Too bad you have to work, Michael, because I'm sure there are tickets available."

"Yeah, too bad." Michael slipped his hands into his trouser pockets, his gaze never leaving Katherine's. "It's a shame the lecture isn't being repeated tomorrow night. I'm sure Bridget, my date, would find it as stimulating as I would. As an international stewardess she doesn't get much of a chance for that type of thing." He shifted his gaze to Katherine's. "If you could hang around you'd meet her. She's coming here straight from the airport."

Bridget? Katherine fumed moments later as she left the bar with Dean. Michael had a date with a stewardess? No doubt Bridget would be too light-headed from so many takeoffs and landings to appreciate a lecture on something as important as the functional art of the Mayas, Olmecs and Aztecs.

She slipped her arm through Dean's and tipped her chin up. She hoped Michael would have fun with his dizzy date, because she was going to have a perfectly wonderful time with hers.

Six

Michael paced. Where the hell was she? She'd left the bar—he checked his watch—six hours and ten minutes ago. He pictured her and Dean strolling out the door arm in arm, and his chest tightened.

He shouldn't have let her go, Michael thought for the hundredth time. He should have leaped over the bar, punched that intellectual bozo out and hauled Katherine into his arms. It certainly was what he'd wanted to do.

Michael flexed his fingers. But he'd had no right to follow his instincts. He had no claim on her, so he'd stood by and let her leave with a man who had sent her flowers on Valentine's Day and asked her to say "yes." Michael cursed and dragged his hands through his hair, his heart thudding against his chest as he pictured Katherine in the other man's arms, in his bed.

He started to pace again. Where was she? It was two o'clock in the morning, for God's sake! He checked his watch, then groaned as he saw it was actually after two. What could they be doing? Activities at this time of the morning were limited. He imagined several of the juicier possibilities and broke out in a cold sweat.

It'd been torture watching her all night. She'd been beautiful, vivacious, alluring; men had been falling all over themselves for her attention. A panicky sensation settled in his stomach. He'd experienced it earlier tonight and he remembered feeling the same way at eighteen when faced with Katherine's brainy friends. or, worse, her parents.

The sensation made him feel young and uncertain, and he strode to the window and glared out at the night. There was no movement on the river; there wasn't a light shining on either shore. Of course there wasn't, he thought derisively, everyone in Rockford except him, Katherine and Dean was home sleeping.

He swung away from the window and stared at the front door, willing it to open, willing Katherine to be on the other side. What had gotten into her? Bars, low-cut sweaters and martinis weren't her style. Neither were provocative glances or throaty laughs. What was she trying to prove, or rather, who was she trying to impress?

Not him, he thought, frustrated. She'd barely looked at him before her professor friend had come in, and not at all after. Michael grinned as he thought of her drink refill and her reaction to it. A moment later his smile faded. There were lots of ways to have fun, and all of them could be had without liquor.

Fun. The panic tightened in his chest, almost overwhelming him. He wanted his old Katie back. His serious, quiet, a little shy Katie. He wanted the woman who was cautious, analytical and covered from head to toe in conservative wools. And he wanted her home.

Michael started to check his watch again, then gritted his teeth and stuffed his hands into his pockets. Watching the clock wasn't going to help—neither was pacing. A drink, he decided, setting his jaw. A drink would help, and several would be even better. Tossing another glance at the door, he headed for the kitchen.

Katherine took a deep breath outside the condominium door, and silently gave thanks she was home. The evening with Dean had been perfect, all right—a perfect disaster. The lecture had been boring—the anthropologist had used as many five-syllable words as possible and delivered them all in a monotone. Dinner had been even worse. Dean had chosen a restaurant as pretentious as the lecture, then had kept up a steady stream of self-aggrandizement. She hadn't been able to get a word in edgewise.

All she'd been able to think about had been Michael and getting home, and the more she'd wanted to leave, the more Dean had lingered. The scenic route back to her condo had been the last straw, and in desperation she'd complained of a headache.

Katherine let her breath out in a long sigh and fitted her key into the lock. She'd seen Michael's car in the lot so she knew he was home. Before she had, she'd been afraid he would still be out; now she was afraid he would be up. She squared her shoulders. If he was, she would give it one last try. She had to.

She turned the key and stepped inside. The apartment was dark save for the light that streamed from the kitchen doorway. She hesitated, then shrugged out of her coat and hung it up. If he wasn't in the kitchen, he was asleep. Hope threaded through her, and she called herself a coward. Pulse racing, Katherine headed for the bright rectangle of light.

He was up. He was wearing blue jeans and a thick white sweater; his feet were bare, his hair rumpled. He was leaning against the sink, staring out the window. There was a full glass of red wine on the counter next to him, an open bottle next to that. He looked at her as she stepped out of the darkness and into the brilliantly lit kitchen.

"Hi," she said, sounding even more nervous than she'd thought she would. She pushed her hair behind her ear; the new shorter layers didn't want to stay there and the inky black strands feathered back over her cheek. "You're still up."

"Evidently." He lifted his glass in a gesture of acknowledgment, then returned his gaze to the window.

She cleared her throat and shifted her weight from her right foot to her left. Something was wrong. It was in his eyes, his stance, his voice. What if that something was Bridget or some other woman?

Katherine realized her hands were trembling and wished for pockets to hide them in. When none appeared, she willed them to be still. This was her chance.

She took a tentative step into the room. "Did the crowd thin out after I left?"

"What crowd?" he asked sarcastically, bringing the glass to his lips, not taking his gaze from the window.

"Is that what's bothering you?" She took another step toward him, relieved. "The kids had—"

"Nothing's bothering me," he interrupted, looking at her then, pinning her with furious eyes. "Is something bothering you?"

She stopped and clasped her hands together. "No, but I—"

"Good night, then."

His dismissal was like a slap in the face. She glared at him. "Aren't you home a little early? I thought you had a date with Bridget." She yanked off her gloves. "Or didn't it get off the ground?"

The corners of his mouth lifted derisively. "Aren't you home a little late? Your lecturer must have been long-winded."

He looked so smug she wanted to hit him. She tossed her gloves on the counter instead. "Not at all. We went out to dinner."

"Dinner, too? My, my, all that excitement in one evening." He turned back to the window and the view of the dark river. "Thai food or German?"

At his mocking tone, Katherine lifted her chin. "Russian, if you must know. And delicious." Michael didn't reply, didn't turn from the window. She stared at his back, seconds ticking past, her temperature rising. She narrowed her eyes. "Dean's an exciting companion, vital and witty. We had a wonderful time."

Michael turned then, his eyes dark and unreadable, his mouth set. He took two steps toward her. "Really? You should have invited him up for more witty, exciting conversation."

"If I'd invited him up," she flung back, "it wouldn't have been for conversation."

Michael took another step; he looked as if he could do murder. "Funny," he said softly, "I would have guessed him a man more interested in himself than in—" he paused, his eyes skimming over her "—making love. Be glad you didn't, Katie. He wouldn't have made you happy."

"How would you know?" she demanded, wanting to sound furious and sounding breathless instead. She tried again. "You are so conceited—"

"Maybe so," Michael murmured, his voice caressing. "But a good lover has eyes only for his woman. He doesn't care about definitive texts, or unnecessary lectures or the right choice of restaurant. He only cares about making his woman happy, can think only about the feel of her skin, the invitation of her perfume, the blue of her eyes."

Dammit, he was right. About the lecture, the restaurant, Dean. She threw her head back angrily. "And you think you're a good lover?"

"I don't think . . . I know."

Prove it. The words jumped to her lips, she swallowed them, shocked. One of them had to stop this— now. Without another word, Katherine turned away from him and started out of the kitchen.

"Nothing to say, Katie?" he mocked. "No comeback? No glowing defense of your new boyfriend?"

She whirled around then, eyes flashing. "Okay." She squared her shoulders in challenge. "I think you're just intimidated by his intellectual capabilities."

For a full ten seconds Michael didn't move a muscle. Then he closed the distance between them, his eyes locked with hers, his expression deadly. When he reached her, he grasped her upper arms and jerked her against his chest. "Repeat that," he said, his voice low, too soft, no longer a caress but a challenge.

She should apologize; she should back down. She tilted her face so their eyes met and clung. The blood thrummed crazily in her head. "You heard me."

The silence crackled between them. Silence and something else. Something primitive, dangerous and out of control. The fine hairs at the back of her neck stood up; every nerve ending throbbed with anticipation. She drew a breath, and the sound was ragged in the otherwise quiet room.

Michael moved his hands up until his fingers splayed in her hair, gripped the back of her head. "Capability this," he muttered a second before his mouth crashed down on hers.

Katherine's head would have fallen back under the force of his kiss, but his hands held her. She dug her fingers into his shoulders, answering his fury with her own. His tongue invaded her mouth, she did battle with it. Teeth scraped, breaths caught, tongues urged.

Michael's hands raced down her back, he cupped her, lifted her, ground himself against her. She twisted her fingers in his hair, the breath rushing past her parted lips, her hips responding with equal force.

When her feet once again touched the ground, Katherine broke the contact, panting, frightened by what she'd done and by the emotions raging through her. Although she hadn't said the words aloud, in every other way she'd challenged Michael—his masculinity, his prowess. She'd wanted to provoke him, had known he wouldn't back down. She had gotten what she'd hoped for.

It wasn't pretty, it wasn't nice. She wasn't proud. And this wasn't the way she wanted him, tonight, ever. Katherine met his eyes. They were dark and wild and somehow young. She took a step back, then another. "Michael, I don't want this . . . it isn't—"

"Isn't what?" he rasped, pulling her back against the hard wall of his chest. "Nice like with your professor?

Or civilized enough for a girl from the right side of the tracks?''

Blood rushed to her cheeks. That he could suggest she would go from one man's arms to another's was like a knife in her heart, that he'd brought up their social differences hurt even more. She flattened her hands against his chest and shoved. When she was free, she lifted her chin haughtily. "What's wrong? Didn't *you* have fun tonight?''

Michael was absolutely still for what seemed like minutes but was in actuality only the space of a heartbeat. When he finally spoke, his voice was even but too soft. "Did you?''

"What do you think?''

Michael flinched. He'd wanted to hear that she'd had a terrible night, instead she'd all but confirmed what he feared. Something snapped inside him, something essential, something that made him whole. And it hurt.

He crossed to her in two steps and cupped her face in his palms. "Tell me,'' he said roughly. "I want to hear you say it.''

His fingers were gentle; there was the capacity for violence in his eyes. "I don't know what you're asking,'' she said coolly, jerking against his grasp. "Now let me go.''

"Not until you tell me.'' He tightened his hold on her. "Did you say yes?''

The question hovered between them. At first Katherine wasn't sure what he meant, then she knew. The flowers, the card. Her pulse fluttered as she met his gaze. "I said no.''

She saw the relief flicker over his face, thought for one wild moment that it mattered to him, that he cared. Then he dropped his hands and walked away from her.

Frustration welled in her chest until she thought she might choke on it. He didn't want another man to touch her, but he didn't want her himself.

Anger replaced frustration, and she raced after him. She caught him as he reached the couch. Grabbing his elbow, she swung him back around. "Would it have mattered to you if I had?"

The question twisted in his gut. In a strange way, it seemed nothing had ever mattered more. "Yes," he said, his voice harsh. "Satisfied?"

He made a move to leave again, and she tightened her fingers on his arm. "Not good enough, Michael. I want to know why."

He stared at her for a long moment. Her eyes were dangerously blue and determined, her cheeks wild with angry color. She was breathtakingly beautiful. There was a quiet but steady ache in his chest, an ache he knew it was best to ignore. Finally, wearily, he said, "We're both tired. Go to bed, Katherine."

He was doing it again—dismissing her! She wouldn't allow it, just as she wouldn't let him play big brother or guardian. Not this time. She met his eyes. "*Why* would it matter, Michael? Why would it matter if I had slept with Dean?"

"Shut up, Ka—"

"Or those guys next to me at the bar?"

He hauled her against his chest, his breath ragged. "Katie..."

"Or if I slept with a different guy every ni—"

Michael caught the words with his mouth. Each had been like a blow to his stomach, and it was the only way he could think of to make her stop. As his lips met hers, as she pressed against him, opening to him, pain and desperation were replaced by heat. White-hot and stinging, raging out of control.

Michael gave in to the heat, welcomed it. He didn't think of the "why" she'd demanded to know, didn't consider the past that had scarred or the future he feared more, he just let the flames engulf him. It seemed like forever since he'd been able to think of anything but Katherine in his arms, burning for him as he did for her.

He felt the anger, the hurt begin to wash out of him, to be replaced by a need so great he thought he might drown in it. Her words had wounded him, cut him in a way no one or nothing else had in years. For a split second he'd been a terrified boy again. And in that second he'd reacted. He hadn't wanted to hurt her; he hadn't wanted to dominate or possess her. He'd wanted her to make him whole again. The way only she could.

Now he just wanted her. All of her. Everything.

Somewhere in the recesses of his mind, Michael acknowledged that this was wrong. He couldn't commit to any woman...especially Katie. Touching her now was chancing hurting her more than she could know.

Even as the thoughts tumbled crazily through his head, he deepened the kiss. He couldn't take the chance, but he couldn't let her go, either. Michael drew her tongue inside him, becoming intoxicated by her taste.

His mouth still locked with hers, he trailed his hands over her neck, shoulders and finally, her breasts. He traced the full curves with the tips of his fingers, then moved on, only to come back again. And again.

Through the thin, soft weave of her sweater, he felt the peaks of her breasts harden with excitement. With a moan, he let his mouth follow his hands until he buried his face in her breasts. She smelled as innocent, as girlish as she had at eighteen. But now she felt like a woman. Round, lush, totally female.

As he bit one tip, then the other, Katherine made a sound of pleasure and arched her back. A wave of desire gripped him, so strong, so sweeping, that for a moment it was all he could do not to drag her to the floor with him, push aside their clothes and enter her. He took a deep breath and tried to garner a modicum of control. He needed to slow down and savor; he was rushing things, he wasn't being fair to Katie. Taking another breath, he loosened his hold on her.

Katherine sensed Michael pulling away and stood on tiptoe, clutched at his shoulders and deepened the kiss. Through his sweater she could feel the tightness of his muscles; she was unsure whether they were rigid with control or the lack of it.

Her calves began to cramp, forcing her to return her heels to the floor. She used the opportunity to explore other rigid places—places that made her dizzy with need, light-headed with awareness. Without thinking, she moved her hand between them until she found him. Even through the denim she felt his heat, his power, and she squeezed.

"God, Katie—" he ground out the words and caught her hand "—you're—"

She pulled her fingers from his. "Don't stop." She arched and moved against. "Not now...if you stop—"

"I won't." He tangled his fingers in her hair, then lowered his mouth to hers once again. The meeting was long, deep, breathtaking. When he lifted his head, he met her eyes. "I couldn't...don't you know that?"

"Then why..." she sighed as he trailed his lips across her cheek to her ear, then nipped the sensitive lobe. "Why did you..."

"I don't want to rush this." Michael drew in a deep, harsh breath, willing away the ache, tamping down the flames. He let the breath out in a shaky sigh and took a step away from her, catching her hands as she reached out to him. "I want to make love with you—slowly, thoroughly." He brought her hands to his mouth and placed a lingering kiss in each palm. "I want to love every part of your body even if it takes three weeks—" he paused, pulling one finger into his mouth until she whimpered, releasing it when she did "—or longer. I want to hold you and taste you and feel you tremble with need." He laced his fingers with hers. "What do you want, Katie?"

Katherine's knees were weak, and she swayed toward him. "I don't want this night to end."

Michael smiled and drew her closer. He feathered kisses over her face—the corner of her lips, the arch of an eyebrow, the tip of her nose. When he was satisfied he'd cherished every feature, he moved lower to the curve of her jaw, the secret places where her pulse hammered, the silky column of her throat.

She tasted like cream; she felt like heaven. Somehow he'd known she would. Somehow, he felt as if he'd tasted her before, felt the silk of her skin and the sweetness of her response another time. But Michael knew he hadn't. Because if he had, he would never have been able to let her go.

Katherine sighed as his hands followed his mouth, searching, savoring, exploring. How could anything so soft be so potent? Each brush of his lips was cataclysmic, each stroke of his hand dizzying. She felt as if her knees might buckle under the force of nothing stronger than the lightest stroke of flesh against flesh.

He knelt in front of her then, and for once Katherine knew how it felt to be taller than him, and she liked it. She wrapped her fingers in his hair, enjoying its texture, then moved her hands from the top of his head over his strong, broad shoulders.

"Turn around, Katherine," he murmured, looking up at her.

With a small shudder, she did as he asked. She trusted him completely; she had known and loved him too long not to. There was a freedom in that, she realized. To trust without reservation, to know a person so well that she could surrender her body with the certainty that it would be touched with absolute respect, to know that he would never willingly hurt her. It wasn't the love she'd wished—even prayed—for, but it was enough.

Michael lifted her hair off her nape, intending to taste her smooth, white skin. He got lost on the way. Her hair slid through and between his fingers, silky and black, and he remembered watching it slide through hers at the bar. Desire curled through him until he thought he might once again lose his tenuous hold on control.

Breathing deeply, he let the oxygen steady him. When he felt he could touch her without charging like a rutting stallion, he placed a series of tiny, openmouthed kisses on the tender skin of her nape and along the curve of her exposed shoulders. Her scent was most potent there, sweet and womanly, and he was reminded of their shared past, of what she meant to him and—absurdly—of the dream he'd had so many years ago.

He smiled. Her sweater buttoned up the back; the buttons were tiny, pearl and offered infinite opportunities. He released the first, then nuzzled the flesh he'd uncovered. Delighting in her quivering response, he released another and another, tasting each time, nudging aside the fuzzy fabric, whispering provocative promises against her back.

Katherine's breath caught as he unfastened the last one, parted the sweater and slid his hands underneath. Even against her own fevered skin his hands were hot.

"At the bar—" he slid his hands around to the front of her and cupped her breasts "—when I realized you weren't wearing a bra—" he moved his hands in slow, maddening strokes "—I went crazy." He trailed his lips over her spine for one last taste, then turned her around to face him. "Crazy with the need to touch you . . . with jealousy."

Katherine smiled in satisfaction. That he'd been jealous made her light-headed, that he could admit it made her love him all the more. She wished she could tell him. Instead she curled her fingers into his thick, dark hair and whispered, "Love me, Michael. I need you."

With a groan, he buried his face in her breasts. Her skin was milky white, but warm and soft like the petals of sunshine-soaked flowers. Her scent, with its subtle contradictions, enveloped him once again and he acknowledged the truth—he'd never known a woman who moved him more. Or a woman who was more perfect.

How could she have forgotten? Katherine wondered dizzily as Michael slid his hands up the back of her legs. Incredible sensations swirled through her, and her eyes fluttered shut. How could she have forgotten the sweetness with which he made love? It had been the same last time—sweet and poignant and earth-shattering. The last time, she thought again, feeling a trace of regret. If only he would remember.

All thoughts vanished and her eyes flew back open as he slid his hands beneath her skirt. She arched and gripped his shoulders as her knees threatened to buckle. His caress made her shudder and then her knees did give.

"Michael . . . I need you . . . inside me."

Her words were no more than a whimper but they unleashed a tidal wave of passion. It rolled over and engulfed him until savoring became an impossible wish and control vanished like cool water on a hot sidewalk. And with control went their clothes. Michael yanked off his sweater as Katherine worked at clinging hosiery. He stepped out of his jeans and tossed them aside; she unzipped her skirt and let it slither to the floor. But when she went for the scrap of lace that hid the last of her from him, he stopped her.

"Let me, Katie." Michael met her eyes and, reading the acquiescence there, trailed his index fingers over the delicate fabric, then hooked his fingers around the top. With infinite care, as if he were opening the present he'd waited for all his life, he slid the panties over her hips and down her legs. His breath lodged in his throat as he looked at her and, without a word, swept her into his arms and carried her to the sofa.

Moments later, his weight pressed her into the cushions and his mouth crashed down on hers. Their tongues met even as their hands urged. His body felt wonderful against hers, hot, strong, demanding. She ran her hands along the corded plane of his back, rubbed her feet against his furred calves, rocked her pelvis against his.

Michael groaned against her lips. He'd wanted to please her more; he'd wanted to make love with her forever. He had no more control.

She curled her legs around him at the same moment she tore her mouth from his. She had to ask again; it wouldn't change a thing, but she had to try. "Why, Michael?" she rasped, clutching at his shoulders, her breasts heaving with the effort it took to stop. His arousal was against her, hot, insistent and exciting. "Why would it matter?"

Michael drew a long, shuddering breath and met her stormy gaze. He couldn't answer her, because he didn't *know* why. He only knew that it mattered so much it hurt and that without her he might never be whole again. Feeling as if he was acting in an absurd play, portraying a part that had been destined for him, knowing in his gut that it would be his downfall but unable to avoid it, he slipped into her. She made a sound of pleasure that was mirrored in her eyes.

They rocked together, hearts hammering, breath short. Katherine moved her hands to the back of his head, tangling her fingers in his thick, dark hair, drawing his mouth to hers; Michael slipped his hands underneath her, bringing her even closer. Their lips muffled each other's cries as they reached for the stars and caught one.

The star was brilliant and warm; the experience brief but magical. Katherine curled up against his side for a moment of perfect contentment before reality set in.

And set in it did—awkward, uncertain, terrifying. Indecision gripped her with a force equal to the desire of a minute ago. Katherine squeezed her eyes shut and drew a deep breath as she acknowledged the truth. This time she couldn't crawl out of bed and slink back to her room to hide. He wasn't drunk or asleep; he would remember. And she had to deal with the consequences of what had just happened between them.

She let out her pent-up breath in a silent sigh and opened her eyes. "Michael, I—"

"Don't say anything, Katie," he said quickly, softly, as he pulled her closer to him. "I feel terrible. I feel . . . Katie—" he drew in a ragged breath "—God, I'm sorry. I didn't mean for this to happen, didn't plan for it to."

For one brief moment she felt nothing, then pain tore through her. In every way, history had been repeated. She'd changed her looks; she'd flirted, teased, provoked. And still nothing had changed.

That wasn't true, she thought, clutching at what was left of her pride. Something had changed. This hadn't been an accident; she hadn't just given in to circumstances. She had made it happen; for once, with Michael, she had controlled her own destiny.

It took everything she had, but she met his eyes. "Don't be sorry. I wanted this with you, only you. I asked for it." She walked her fingers up his chest with a playfulness she was far from feeling. "After all, a girl has to be discriminating about whom she has an affair with."

For a full minute Michael was quiet. When he finally spoke, his husky voice didn't give a clue to how he felt. "Is that so?"

"Mmm-hmm . . ." She worked to sound sophisticated. "Why settle for less than the best?"

"The best," he murmured almost to himself, trailing his fingers through her hair. "I'm flattered but not sure I'm up to the job."

His words cut like paper—thin, deep and stinging. This was it? One night? He wasn't even interested in an affair with her? Tonight was no different than twelve years ago, only now she couldn't blame booze or youth or her own ineptness. Tears welled in her eyes; she furiously blinked them away. She would not cry over Michael Tardo! She'd given it a shot; she could hold her head up and say she'd tried.

"Come on, Michael," she said, attempting a light tone and achieving a brittle one. "You're the one who described yourself as a wonderful lover."

"True." Michael tightened his fingers in her hair, then relaxed them until the inky strands feathered through his fingers. "And tonight, right or wrong, mistake or not, we're lovers. So. . ."

Before she had time to catch her breath, he'd captured both of her hands in one of his and hauled them over her head. She met his gaze as evenly as he met hers. "So?" she prompted, her voice no more than a whisper.

He raked his gaze slowly over her, then returned it to her face. "There's still—" he lowered his head "—a little—" he made a warm, wet path across her breasts "—night left."

Heat crept over her until she thought she must glow from it. There was no chance for permanency; he didn't even want an affair; she should stop this now. "Michael—"

"No," he murmured, trailing the fingers of his free hand over her. "No talking. There'll be plenty of time tomorrow for that. Tonight—" he ran the flat of his hand over her abdomen, then lower "—is only for this." He found her, hot and moist, and she arched against him.

"Michael—" she let out her breath slowly "—stop that."

"Stop what?" He leaned down, his mouth hovering a fraction from hers. He moved his fingers. "This?"

When she bit back a moan, he enticed her again. "Or this?"

"No...yes. I think...I'd like to..." All thoughts of stopping flew out of her mind as slow strokes became maddening circles.

"Cat got your tongue, Katie?" He nipped at her bottom lip, catching it, pulling it slowly into his mouth.

"Oh..." He finally released her hands, but she used them for pulling closer instead of pushing away. She clung to him until everything disappeared but the sensations rocketing through her.

When her pulse had finally slowed, when she felt she could once again think coherently, she turned to him, smiling lazily. "As you said, tonight is only for...this." Before he realized what she meant, she'd captured him.

Seven

Michael was gone. Confused, disoriented, Katherine sat up in bed and pushed the tangle of hair out of her eyes. She scanned the room. Judging by the slant of the light through the windows it wasn't much past seven; she was alone. A thread of panic tightened in her stomach, and she tried to push away her sudden fear.

He was probably making coffee, she told herself, throwing back the blankets and getting out of bed. Or reading the paper. Sure. He was here. He wouldn't have left without saying anything. She pulled on her robe, stepped into her slippers and went out to look for him.

The house was still, cold, empty. Katherine stopped in the kitchen, noting that he hadn't even taken the time for a cup of coffee. He'd wanted to get out fast, she thought, taking perverse pleasure in the way that truth twisted in her gut.

She crossed to the coffeepot, filled it with water, measured out the grounds, then plugged it in. As she turned to leave the room, her gaze lighted on the gloves she'd tossed on the counter the night before as she'd angrily faced Michael. Near them was Michael's still-full glass of wine. She stared at the objects, her eyes misting over. Empty gloves, untouched wine—a barren still life, a still life that mirrored the way she felt inside.

Sucking in a determined breath, she crossed to the gloves and picked them up. The leather was cold but soft against her palms, and she held on to them tightly. Why was she surprised by Michael's desertion? There was no reason for her to be hurt. He'd made his feelings perfectly clear last night; why had she expected them to be any different in the harsh light of day?

No melodrama, Katherine told herself, curling her fingers around the supple leather. No anger, no disillusionment. She'd taken her chance; she'd known the odds going in. She would accept what happened and start to build the rest of her life.

Squaring her shoulders, Katherine went to her coat and tucked her gloves into its pocket. She would have a nice, quiet Sunday, she told herself. She would enjoy a leisurely breakfast while she read the paper, then she would dress and maybe do a little shopping. Sure. It would be perfect.

Ignoring the hollow feeling in the pit of her stomach, she opened the front door to retrieve the paper. It was there and she plucked it up, then, unable to help herself, moved to the window that looked out over the parking lot. She was being silly. The parking lot wouldn't tell her any more about where— Her breath caught. Michael's car wasn't gone—and neither was he.

He was standing beside his restored Corvette talking with a woman.

A young woman, Katherine thought, feeling a tightness in her throat. Even from this distance she could see that the girl was beautiful: tall, with long blond hair and a willowy figure.

As Katherine watched, the girl placed her hands on Michael's shoulders and looked adoringly up at him. The tightness in Katherine's throat moved to her chest, and she whirled around and raced back inside.

She didn't stop until she'd reached the kitchen and the louvered door had swung closed behind her. Her whole body shaking, she sagged against the counter. She wasn't certain how long she stood there, refusing to think, refusing to acknowledge what she'd seen. Michael had left her bed to go to another woman.

Finally, she drew in a deep, shuddering breath and pulled herself erect. She stared out the window, hurt ballooning inside her. Maybe it was a mistake. Maybe he—

"You're up."

Katherine spun around in surprise. Michael was standing in the doorway, his face flushed from the cold, his hair spiky from his own fingers. As he shrugged out of his jacket he met her eyes. In them she read regret, concern, guilt. And in that instant, she felt exactly as she had twelve years ago. Funny—a few months ago, she wouldn't have believed she could ever feel that raw, that vulnerable again.

She straightened her spine, suddenly as furious as she was hurt. "Shouldn't I be?"

Michael met her eyes and wished he could turn the clock back twenty-four hours. There was a catch in his chest, and he shoved his hands into the pockets of his jeans. "No. It was just that you were—"

"Sleeping so soundly when you left," she finished for him, her voice cold.

"Yes."

She turned back to the window. "Convenient."

He lowered his brows. "What's that supposed to mean?"

"Nothing." Katherine realized she was gripping the counter so tightly the edge was cutting into her hands and relaxed her grip.

He'd hurt her, Michael thought, searching her expression. He didn't know—and couldn't allow himself to wonder—how she felt about him, but his leaving while she still slept had hurt her. He longed to pull her into his arms and soothe her; he pushed the longing away. This was the way it had to be.

He stared at her set profile and sighed. "I'm sorry."

His apology ripped through her; Katherine met his eyes evenly anyway. "For what?"

"For . . . everything."

Anger shot through her. He couldn't even admit the truth out loud—that he regretted they'd made love, that he'd gone to another woman, that he'd left her alone after the night they'd shared. Well, she wouldn't hide or pretend. Not this time.

"I'd think that even with the one-night stand crowd a note or a goodbye is expected after a night like ours."

What could he say to her? That he'd needed to think, to plan how he could cut her quickly and efficiently out of his life? He looked away. "I was wrong; I shouldn't have left without talking to you."

When she only looked at him, he stretched a hand out to her. "Katie, I feel like a real jerk. I'm sorry. Last night shouldn't have—"

"Don't say anything else!" she interrupted, whirling around to face him. "And for God's sake, no more apologies! We went through this last night. There's no reason for you to feel guilty. Nothing happened that I didn't want to, that I didn't ask for."

He crossed his arms over his chest to keep from reaching for her. "But I knew going in that I couldn't give you anything, Katie. You didn't. That wasn't fair."

Bitterness rose like bile in her throat. She'd known it all along—she'd just refused to believe it. "Don't flatter yourself, Michael. You don't know what I'm thinking or what I want." She angled her chin defiantly. "I had fun. If you remember, that's what I'd set out to do."

Her words twisted in his gut. He wanted to haul her against his chest and kiss her until she admitted she felt more than that, that last night had been as special to her as to him. He reminded himself that he was the kind of man who could desert a sleeping woman and turned away from her. "Great. I had fun, too."

"Good." She dumped his glass of wine from the night before in the sink. "I'm glad that's settled. I'm going to dress." As she brushed by him, he caught her arm. She met his eyes.

Michael stared at her, and the memory of what her arms had felt like around him, holding him, pulling him closer as he moved into her, swamped his senses. "Dammit, Katie. We're friends. Let's not throw that away."

"Don't worry, Michael." She laughed; the sound was cool and tight. "I don't feel any differently than I did before last night, or for that matter, than I did twelve years ago.''

Michael's gaze searched her face. Her cheeks were the color of the small pink flowers that grew wild at the side of the road, her eyes the flawless blue of the Mediterranean. And she was telling the truth. She felt the same as she always had; last night hadn't meant more to her than "fun." Terrific. Great. It was what he wanted, too.

Ignoring the knot in his chest, Michael lowered his eyes to her mouth. It was set but still soft; the need to kiss her rushed over him like wildfire. He wanted to press his mouth to hers and feel it moisten and part under his, wanted to soothe, excite, possess. He wanted to prove this thing between them was so much more than "fun."

He couldn't afford to touch her again. Ever.

He dropped his hand, and she started toward the door. Just as she reached it, he said, "We've been invited to a party."

Katherine stopped but didn't turn around. "When?" she asked, even though she had no intention of going, no matter when it was being held.

"Next Saturday night."

"I have plans."

He clenched his fists. With Dean? "Break them."

She turned back to him then, furious. "I don't think so. We're not dating, Michael. Go without me."

"No," he said softly, dangerously. "It's Sam Steele's fiftieth birthday and we've been invited. What would Susi think if I came without you?"

Katherine tossed her head back. "I don't care."

"Well, I do." Michael pinned her with his gaze. "You made a deal, Katie. I agreed to become your study partner, and you agreed to pretend to be my lover."

"And you promised my bedroom door would stay closed," she shot back, knowing it would hurt him and wanting him to experience just a modicum of what she was feeling.

Michael took a step toward her. "Your bedroom door did stay closed, Katie. Surely you remember your impatience—" he swept his eyes slowly over her, before meeting hers once again "—or should I refresh your memory?"

Chills raced up her arms. She told herself anger caused them; she knew better. It was the picture Michael's words had elicited—the white couch, their hastily discarded clothes, pillows thrown aside in a frenzy. She and Michael—breast to breast, lips clinging, crisp hair against smooth skin. His breath against her ear—hot and ragged, her hands against his flesh—urgent, demanding.

"Don't bother," she snapped, realizing her heart was beating fast and her breath was short. "I have a memory."

He folded his arms across his chest. "So, are you going to hold up your end of the bargain?"

Katherine gritted her teeth. He knew her and her damnable sense of fair play too well. "Fine," she snapped. "What time?"

"Seven-thirty."

Without acknowledging him in any way, she left the kitchen.

The night of the party arrived, despite Katherine's wish that it hadn't. While Michael checked their coats, she nervously smoothed her sweater-dress over her hips. It was straight, unadorned and the color of elderberries. The soft, wide leather belt at her waist was the same color as the dress, as were her pumps.

The dress was a perfect choice for a party being held at the Wagon Wheel Lodge in Rocton. The resort was designed with an Old-West motif, and this building was a replica of a dance hall, complete with wagon-wheel light fixtures, polished wood floor and exposed log beams. The atmosphere was suited to loud music and laughter, or warm drinks and cozy conversations in front of the huge stone fireplace.

She was in the mood for neither, Katherine thought, resisting the urge to smooth her dress yet again. She shot an irritated glance over her shoulder at Michael. He looked relaxed, even pleased with himself. She stiffened her spine. She resented the fact that he'd maneuvered her into accompanying him tonight by playing upon her overdeveloped sense of responsibility. She scowled. And it was that same sense of responsibility that wouldn't allow her *not* to act the part of Michael's lover. But she didn't have to like it, she vowed, turning to him as he came up beside her.

He laid a possessive hand against the small of her back, and Katherine stiffened. "We don't have an audience, Michael," she said coolly, stepping away from his touch. "So hands off."

Michael narrowed his eyes and closed the tiny gap she'd made between them. He cupped her face in his palms. "Still angry about having to change your plans? Would it help if I said I was sorry?"

She drew in a sharp breath at his tone. He was patronizing her! "No," she whispered angrily, trying to ignore her racing heart. "Now let me go."

He brought his hand up to cup her other cheek. The curve of his lips was wicked. "Oh look, here comes Susi."

"Michael, don't—"

"The perfect audience," he continued, trailing his thumb across her flushed cheek.

"—you dare. I mean it, Michael."

"So do I." His lips hovered above hers. "Look in love, Katie."

Katherine flattened her hands against his chest as his mouth settled over hers. She meant to push him away but his mouth was warm and familiar, his taste as heady, as potent as fine old brandy. She curled her fingers into his lapels and gave herself over to his kiss.

And a moment after she did, Michael lifted his head. "She's gone," he whispered, his lips still only a fraction from hers.

"Mmm." Katherine's eyes fluttered open.

He smiled down at her. "You can let go of my jacket now. But you don't have to. In fact, I prefer my women draped over me."

Katherine jerked away from him as if stung. She tossed her head. "Don't flatter yourself. I said I would play this damn part and—"

"Only playing a part?" Michael reached out and wound a piece of her ebony hair around his finger. "You missed your calling, then. You're a hell of an actress."

She wanted to hit him because he was right. She lifted her chin instead. "I see lack of ego still isn't a problem. You'll never change, Michael."

"So I've been told." He dropped his hand and held out his arm. "But there's something to be said for knowing what you are. Don't you think?"

Katherine gritted her teeth. Her comments—now and eight years ago—just bounced off him. But his, as always, sliced clear to her soul. "I think I'd like to get this over with."

He laughed and tucked her arm through his. "Careful, Katie, you don't want to seem too eager. After all, I'm sure we'll have to...pretend...often tonight."

Katherine's stinging reply was cut off as they stepped into the throng of partiers.

After an hour of trying to keep up with Michael, Katherine was ready for a quiet corner. She found that and a glass of ice-cold punch and gratefully melted into the woodwork. She took a long swallow of the drink—it was a refreshing combination of fruit juices, rum and sparkling water—and sighed. She'd forgotten how Michael thrived on parties...and how she hated them.

She took another sip of the punch and frowned. Michael was the one with the acting ability. He deserved an Academy-Award nomination for the way he'd treated her over the past hour. He'd been solicitous, attentive...even loving. Her heart tripled its beat, and she pulled her eyebrows together and took another sip of punch. It had been as if...as if he really wanted to be her lover. Katherine smiled to herself. That was the silly imagining of a woman too used to deluding herself.

"You have a lovely smile, much like the Mona Lisa's. Shame to waste it."

Katherine jumped and the last of her punch sloshed over the rim of her cup. Luckily there wasn't enough left to do any damage, and she mopped most of it up with her cocktail napkin. That done, she turned toward the man who had come up beside her. He was big and handsome, with thick, silver hair and bushy eyebrows.

He was holding out a full glass of punch and wearing a contrite expression.

"Sorry about that. Here, have another." When she hesitated, he added, "Go on, I hate the stuff. My metabolism needs something with a little more kick."

Katherine returned his smile and took the glass. "Thank you. But you're missing out, it's delicious."

"Humph. That's what the wife said." He looked over his shoulder as if to confirm they were alone, then back at her. "Getting old is a pain in the butt. The wife won't let me have cigars, whiskey or what she calls 'fatty meat.' You'd think when a man reaches his golden years he'd be allowed a little fun."

Katherine laughed and shook her head. "Golden years, my foot. And it sounds to me as if your wife loves you very much."

He snorted again but the smile tugging at his mouth gave him away. "So...you're Michael's woman."

Katherine choked on her punch, and he slapped her on the back. When she caught her breath, she looked up at him with watery eyes. "Have we met?"

"We haven't. Somebody needs to teach that boy some manners. Can't even pay his respects to an old man on his birthda—"

"You're Sam Steele." Smiling warmly, Katherine fitted her hand to his. "Michael has talked of you often. Happy birthday." When he didn't reply, just continued to inspect her with lively, curious eyes, she shifted and tried again. "It's a lovely party."

He grunted, waving aside the pleasantries. "Parties are a pain in the butt, too. Besides, I'm not standing here to talk about watery punch or birthday parties. Let me get a look at you; you're not what I expected."

Katherine smiled even as she felt heat climb up her cheeks. Sam Steele was gruff to the point of rudeness but she liked him anyway. "What did you expect?" she asked dryly. "A bimbo?"

Sam's bushy eyebrows shot up for a moment before he burst out laughing. "You've got a smart mouth for such a little thing. It would take a woman with a sharp tongue and a quick wit to get by all that boy's blarney."

Her lips twitched in amusement. She suspected Mr. Steele had plenty of the blarney himself. "Thanks. I manage to hold my own."

Sam nodded his head in Michael's direction. "I'm surprised Michael settled down at all."

Katherine followed Sam's gaze. Michael's face was animated and as he said something, the group of people gathered around him—the majority of whom were women—burst out laughing. She acknowledged feeling a twinge; she would be surprised, too, if it ever happened.

"I've known Michael all his life," Sam continued. "In fact, visited him and his mama in the hospital the day after he was born."

"Then you knew—"

"His father," Sam finished for her, patting his vest pockets. "I grew up next to Michael's mother; our families were close. Never did understand what little Mary Sciame saw in Anthony Tardo. He was as wild as she was quiet, as worldly as she was innocent." He found what he was looking for and, sending Katherine a conspiratorial glance, pulled a cigar out of his pocket. "That's not completely true, Anthony was a handsome devil and such a charmer... just like Michael." Sam shook his head. "I remember the day they met;

Mary took one look and fell madly in love. There was never anyone else for her.''

Katherine swallowed. This story was too familiar. ''What happened?''

''He got her pregnant and agreed—not without some help from both their families—to do the right thing.'' Sam nipped the end of his cigar, then lit it. ''Forcing them to marry never made any sense to me; they were the most unlikely couple. Of course, times were different.''

The most unlikely couple. Katherine repeated the phrase to herself, lowering her eyes to her punch. Like her and Michael. After a moment, she looked back at Sam. ''He walked out on them when Michael was six.''

''Mmm.'' He puffed on his cigar. ''It practically killed her. She was better off without him, though. He was never faithful, hardly ever home—a real rover.'' He blew out a cloud of smoke. ''He even worked for me for a while, but it didn't last.'' Sam's gaze strayed back to Michael. ''I can't believe how alike they are. Everyone always said so. Even Mary.''

The fine hairs at the back of her neck stood up and Katherine tore her eyes from Michael to look back at Sam. ''Pardon?''

''How alike.'' Sam gestured. ''Michael and his father.''

Katherine stiffened. ''Excuse me—I never met the man, but I know for a fact Michael's nothing like him. Michael cares about people and their feelings. He's honorable and honest. He always has been.''

Sam stared at her in surprise. ''You're right, of course. I meant how much they looked alike.''

The color in her cheeks went from indignant to embarrassed—she couldn't believe how she'd lashed out at the poor man. She shook her head. But there was something about what he'd said, something that plucked at her, but she couldn't quite put her finger on it. The feeling wouldn't go away, and she turned apologetically to Sam. "I didn't know about the... resemblance."

Sam continued to look at Michael. "It was uncanny... it still catches us all off guard sometimes. We look at Michael and see Anthony at the same age. It became harder on Mary as Michael got older. Then when he started to run wild—" Sam stopped abruptly and shook his head. "That's all in the past. I couldn't be prouder of the way Michael's turned out." He was quiet for a moment as he turned and gazed at her. "I'm happy he chose you. Every man needs a woman who believes in him, who's his champion."

Katherine didn't lower her eyes. "I do believe in Michael. I always have."

"Good." Sam puffed on his cigar for several seconds in silence, then surprised her again. "Speaking of how kids turn out... I hope Susi hasn't been making a pest of herself."

Katherine coughed and almost spilled her punch for the second time.

"You don't have to pretend, I know about my daughter's crush on Michael. I haven't known what to do about it so I haven't done anything." He shot her a glance that was part amusement and part apology out of the corner of his eye. "I also know she's a lot like me and can be too... self-assertive. She hasn't caused you or Michael any trouble?"

Katherine thought of the things Michael had told her about Susi and drained her second cup of punch. "Of course not."

Sam chuckled. "A good liar can be an asset to a man in social situations. You take Michael there—uh-oh, here comes my wife, Lily. If she catches me with this cigar..."

"You can hide behind me," Katherine said sweetly, her expression innocent.

Sam glowered as he stamped out his cigar. "You've got a smart mouth, little gal. And a good idea." He held out his arm. "May I have this dance?"

"I'd be delighted," she said, hoping a dance would work off the effect of the deceptively fruity punch. Smiling, she took his arm.

Eight

Michael watched Sam lead Katherine onto the dance floor and frowned. What had that little scene when they'd first arrived been all about? He'd acted like an idiot, had done exactly the opposite of what he knew he should. He should have been glad she was angry with him, been relieved if she didn't want him near her. He should have tried to convince himself they were just friends, that the other night had been no more than physical need, a release of sexual energy or two old friends fulfilling a forbidden fantasy. And the whole time all he'd been able to think about was touching her and proving their time together had been anything but any of those things. What was wrong with him?

He turned his attention back to the woman standing to his right. She was a tall, willowy brunette who worked for the *Register Star* and was obviously interested in doing more with him than talk. Without interest, he mumbled an appropriate response to her question, then, unable to keep his eyes off Katherine, glanced back at her and Sam.

She looked beautiful, he thought, his gaze roaming over her. Her mass of dark hair fell softly to her shoulders and brushed them as she moved; her skin was milky-white and flawless. He caught his breath as she tipped back her head to look up at Sam, the slender column of her throat arching with the movement. His gaze lingered on the enticing curve, and he imagined his lips traveling over the sensitive flesh until he found the pulse point behind her ear—he would stroke; it would throb.

Swallowing hard, Michael lowered his eyes. Her dress was simple but stunning and skimmed her body, giving only hints of the tempting curves beneath; her one piece of jewelry was an antique cameo at her throat. He tipped his head to the side. She wasn't flashy or exotic or mysterious, nor was she anything like the women out of his past. She was small and soft and lovely—and she was his.

Michael drew his dark eyebrows together. This was crazy; it had to stop. She wasn't "his," nor did he care if she was or wasn't his type. It made no difference to him if she *was* the most beautiful woman in the room or if... He craned his neck as she and Sam moved beyond his line of vision. When he caught sight of her again, she was laughing. A twinge started in the pit of his stomach and spread. Michael silently swore. This whole situation had gotten way out of control. Now, along with every other man in the room between the ages of seven and seventy, he was jealous of an old and trusted friend.

"I'd like to interview you at the bar. I'm doing a story on local college hangouts and the people who run them. I think Michael's should be included."

Michael jerked his gaze back to the reporter. "I'm sorry—what were you saying?" Even as the woman started repeating herself, his gaze strayed back to Katherine. She was saying something to Sam and gesturing with her free hand as she did. Mesmerized, he stared at the movement of her fingers, then, realizing what he was doing, jerked his gaze away. Enough was enough. Starting now he was getting smart. No more fantasies that included sweat socks and flannel gowns, no more watching her like a protective lover and, for God's sake, no more touching.

He scowled as her laughter drew the admiring eyes of several men. "Excuse me, will you? There's someone I need to talk to."

Without another glance at the startled reporter, Michael began to pick his way across the dance floor. When he reached the couple, he tapped Sam on the shoulder. "You old war-horse! Are you trying to steal my woman?"

Sam delivered him a deadpan stare. "Seems to me when a man leaves his lady unattended like that, he deserves to have her stolen." Sam whirled Katherine around.

Michael narrowed his eyes and followed. "I'm cutting in."

Sam smiled. "Go tell strangers some more of your bad jokes. Katherine and I are having a fine time."

"A fine time," Katherine repeated, laughing.

Michael sent her a smoldering look. Her cheeks were pink, her eyes twinkling—she'd had too much punch. He supposed he should be grateful she had stayed away

from martinis. Not feeling grateful at all, he tapped
Sam's shoulder once again. "Is that one of your nasty
old stogies I smell?" He made a great show of sniffing.
"I'm sure Lily would be interested—"

"Blackmail?" Sam interrupted, stopping in his tracks
and looking outraged. "I should have had you arrested
when I had the chance!"

Michael grinned. "Well, you missed it. Hand over my
woman."

Sam returned the grin and released her. "To hand this
flower over to a hooligan like yourself is—"

"Put a lid on it, Steele." Michael pulled Katherine
into his arms. "They're playing our song."

Moments later, Katherine and Michael were in the
midst of the dancers. Katherine sighed and melted
against him. She should have been angry; she should
have been stiff in his arms; she hadn't an ounce of resistance in her. It was the rum, she told herself. The
rum, the too-warm room, the sultry music.

She looked up at him and smiled. "'Hand over my
woman?' Don't you think that's a little too macho, even
for you?"

Michael tightened his fingers. Katherine was so tiny
his hands could easily span her waist; even when she was
in heels he could rest his chin on the top of her head.
She was petite, delicate, womanly. The primitive drive
to protect and possess surged through him, and suddenly the memory of past pain and the fear of future
ones disappeared until all that was left was the moment
and its sensations. "No," he murmured, pressing her to
him.

Her pulse fluttered, and Katherine raised her head so
she could see his face. He met her eyes. There wasn't
laughter there or even the usual amusement. Instead, his

dark gaze was hot and fierce. Fluttering gave way to breathlessness, and she dropped her eyes. She was imagining things. She had to be. Katherine squeezed her eyes shut. He was just making up to her for... He rubbed his cheek against her hair and her mind went blank.

"Have I told you how beautiful you look tonight?"

Even though she knew she should make light of the comment, she tilted her head coquettishly. "Not yet."

He laughed low in his throat. "Well, you do. You look soft and sultry, conservative and naughty." He trailed his fingers across her shoulders. "When did you exchange the Coke bottles for contacts?"

"Graduate school." She cleared her throat and prayed for lucidity. The way he was looking at her was scrambling her brain. "I realized I was only wearing them out of...habit and—" she cleared her throat again "—because they made me feel safe."

"You were right," he murmured. "If you'd changed sooner, I would have had to fight off every rake on campus."

Katherine took a deep breath in the hope that the oxygen would help keep her firmly planted in reality. It didn't. "To protect the virtue of Saint Katie?"

"No way. My motives would have been far more selfish."

His smile was wicked with possibilities, and practical reminders and good sense were lost as desire hit her with the force of a sledgehammer. Images followed—images of her and Michael, naked, impatient, straining against one another, searching with hands and tongues and... Katherine pressed her palms against the soft fabric of his jacket, the dizzying sensations sweeping over her.

"You do crazy things to my head, Katie." He brushed his lips across her forehead. "Things I'd do best to ignore."

"Oh?" Katherine ran her hands up his lapels, her eyes meeting his. "Why?"

"Because you're dangerous," he answered softly.

The music quickened and Michael spun her around. She curled her fingers around his shoulders. "You used to like danger."

He laughed. "And you used to be shy." When she blushed, he laughed again and touched a finger to her fevered cheek. "I'm glad this hasn't changed. I was always intrigued by the way your skin could go from milk to rose to flame in a matter of seconds." Her blush deepened. "Like now."

"The curse of my fair-skinned ancestors," she murmured, feeling herself becoming pinker by the second.

He leaned closer and pressed his lips to her ear. "I wish I could thank those ancestors. You blush charmingly in other places, too." He nipped. "Places even more tempting than the ones everybody sees."

Katherine breathed deeply and searched for something to say—something witty, something casual and sophisticated. But all she could think of were warm, rosy places and the reasons for them.

"Isn't there anything about me that you've always admired?" He found the pulse throbbing behind her ear and nuzzled it. "Anything you'd like to tell me about?"

It took her a moment to gather enough breath to speak. When she did, her voice was thick. "Fishing for compliments?"

"You bet."

She looked back up at him, drinking in his face. There were so many things: the way his dark hair curled wildly when wet; or the way his right cheek dimpled, just a little, when he smiled; or the way her name sounded on his lips when they made love. But all those things were physical, and what she admired about Michael went so much deeper than that.

"I've always admired your ability to make friends," she said finally, softly. "I've admired your ease at handling things like this." She paused. "Everyone likes you, Michael. Right off, without hesitation. How do you do it?"

"Like your skin—" he swung her around "—I inherited it."

Another person would have missed the edge in his voice; she didn't. "You don't sound as if you appreciate the gene."

"The party gene." He smiled tightly. "I suppose I ought to be grateful—it's what makes me a good bartender."

"I wish I'd gotten it."

"Still hate parties?" He smiled as he toyed with the tips of her hair that brushed her nape.

"Only ones where I don't know anybody. Generally, I avoid them."

Michael laughed and moved closer. "Just pretend everybody is naked," he whispered. "That's what I do."

His breath was warm against her ear and a tingle raced up her spine. "You're insane."

"Another quality genetic characteristic."

Katherine looked up at him, a small frown forming between her brows. "We sociologists believe that who we are has more to do with environment and experiences than genes. I like the idea of being in control, being able to shape myself and my destiny. The idea of personality being determined at birth—of being a pawn of sorts—has always seemed defeatist and depressing to me."

Michael smiled and ran his index finger along the tiny furrow in her brow, smoothing it. "Whatever it is, we remain true to form. Even in my arms you're the serious little scientist."

She answered his smile with one of her own. "And you're being an irreverent scoundrel."

"Of course." He brought her hand to his lips and pressed a light kiss on her knuckles. "Do you remember the frat party I dragged you to where everyone got smashed and the police came? You were furious."

She laughed up at him. "You dragged me to hundreds of those! I never could convince you that I was happier at home, studying."

Still holding her hand to his lips, Michael met her eyes. "I couldn't stand the thought of you at home alone on a Saturday night. I worried about you."

A lump formed in her throat; she tried to swallow past it. If she had been completely out of her mind, she might have imagined that was tenderness she saw in his eyes. If she'd been a total masochist, she would have called it love. She was neither. "You only had to worry about me when I was with you. You got me into jams I couldn't have even imagined on my own."

"I was a very bad influence, wasn't I?" Michael pulled her even closer and brushed his lips across the top of her head. Her scent was overpowering despite its subtlety, and he drew the perfume in, letting it swamp his senses, growing drunk on its delicacy. "I'm not proud of my past, Katie. I don't like to think about it."

Katherine rubbed her chin lightly against his throat. She caught the tang of spicy soap, enjoyed the rasp of his rough skin against her smooth one. "It doesn't matter what you were, it's what you've become that's important. Surely you know that."

Michael smiled against her hair. Always optimistic, always his champion. He gathered her to him. She couldn't know that people never changed, that they only tempered or modified their behavior. Nor could she realize that the past could hound a person like a trained dog. There was nothing in her experience to teach that lesson. "You saw me at my worst—yet you still believed in me. How could any woman be so perfect?" He smiled. "'Saint Katie'—I think I like the sound of that."

She didn't. It brought to mind virginal white and big, lonely beds. It brought to mind the kind of woman Michael would never choose. "I think all that starch in the collar would start to itch."

Michael laughed. "Oh, Katie…" His voice trailed off as he gazed at her upturned face. Her lashes were thick and coal black, her irises the perfect blue-violet of a periwinkle flower, and her mouth, full and crimson, seemed to beg for his. He thought of soft, fuzzy fabric and smooth, white skin.

Reminding himself of what he should do, he slowed his steps until they only swayed to the music's long, liquid notes. "The band's taking a break," he whispered against her ear, slowing until they moved not at all, just stood at the center of the dance floor, holding each other. "What would you like to do now?"

What she would like to do had her tingling all over. What she should do wasn't even in the running. Katherine looked up at him, smiled and suggested a glass of punch.

For the rest of the night, Michael didn't stray from her side. They danced, laughed and shared too much of the fruity punch; they whispered in each other's ears like schoolchildren . . . or lovers.

It was well past midnight by the time she and Michael said their final goodbyes to Sam and Lily, then stepped out into the clear, black night.

"How about a walk?" Michael asked, putting an arm around her. "It's a pretty night."

"Yes." Katherine nestled against him. "I can't believe it, but I'm not tired."

Michael laughed. "It's the punch."

It wasn't, but Katherine didn't bother to correct him. For a time they walked along the wooden walkways, past the storefronts fashioned to look like the main street of Dodge City or some other frontier town. Through the tall pines, the sky was sprinkled with stars, and each time they exhaled, their breath made a frosty pillow on the night air.

Michael stopped outside a sweet shop designed like a log cabin. "How about an ice cream cone?"

"Michael, it's below freezing out here!"

"I bet they have Rocky Road. You could have a double scoop."

He'd remembered her favorite. Pleased, Katherine peeked through the window. "They're closed."

"There are ways around that." When she arched her eyebrows dubiously, he pulled a credit card out of his wallet and waved it in front of her. "We could leave money."

Katherine thought of how he'd jimmied her dorm-room door all those years ago and her eyes widened. "You wouldn't?"

"How bad do you want ice cream?"

She leaned against him and laughed. "Not badly enough to send you back to a life of crime. I'd never forgive myself. Come on." She grabbed his hand and pulled him toward a covered bridge that spanned a trickle of a stream, now frozen. Once underneath, she smiled up at him. "Safe from temptation."

"Hardly," Michael murmured almost to himself, cupping her face in his hands. "Your teeth are chattering."

Her breath mingled with his. "Your nose is red."

"That's because it's frozen." He leaned forward and rubbed the tip of his against hers, Eskimo style. "I think it's beginning to thaw."

"Good." She placed her gloved hands against the lapels of his camel hair coat. "We wouldn't want it to fall off."

"Certainly not." He lowered his eyes to her lips. "Now all we have to do is get your teeth to stop chattering."

She leaned toward him, just a fraction. "How do you propose we do that?"

"Like this." He lowered his mouth to hers. Her lips were cold, but only for a moment. They warmed, then parted. She tasted of the fruity punch; she held nothing back. Michael groaned as her tongue darted out to catch his, as she sighed and sagged against him. Her body fit perfectly to his and even through the layers of outer garments he could feel the rapid beat of her heart and the way her nipples had tightened with excitement. Or was that his imagination? When it came to Katie, he realized, reality and fantasy melded until he couldn't discern one from the other.

Lifting his head, he gazed at her upturned face. Her eyes were still tightly closed and she was smiling. It was the smile that brought him back to earth. It was soft and sweet and too trusting. Trust. Michael trailed a finger over her right eyebrow and down the curve of her cheek. The air was so cold, yet her skin was so warm. He thought of the past, of history, and consequently, of the future. Futility left a bitter taste in his mouth. "Your teeth stopped chattering," he murmured, his voice sounding thick even to his own ears.

"Mmm..." She came back to reality slowly, easing into it with no will of her own. Her lids fluttered up. "I'm not cold anymore."

Her cheeks were pink from the wind, her eyes dark with arousal. She looked impossibly beautiful. "We should go," he said roughly, setting her away from him.

Katherine moved back to him, sliding her hands up his chest to his shoulders. "I'd rather stay."

"No, Katie." He caught her hands quickly, before he could change his mind. "Enough. We played our little roles tonight, we had a good time. Let's stop it here."

His words hit her like a battering ram. Katherine reeled away from him, hurt. And in that split second between the words registering and being absorbed, hurt transformed to anger, anger to fury. She turned to him in challenge—she would be damned if she would let him treat her like a yo-yo. "Why, Michael?" With a quick, jerky motion, she pushed the hair away from her face. "You were right, we *were* having a good time. Why stop now?"

"Because—" he stuffed his hands into his coat pockets "—I don't have anything to give you."

She felt as if he'd slapped her; she fought the urge to slap him back. "You keep talking about what you have to give me—has it ever occurred to you that maybe I don't want anything? That maybe what we had the other night was enough?''

"No.'' He reached out to touch her, then dropped his hand. "You're a woman who needs commitments, promises. We both know that.''

"Do we?'' She spun away from him, crossing to the opposite railing. She stared down at the frozen stream for a moment, then looked back at him. "Well, here's a news flash, Michael Tardo, all I want from you is a good time. Some fun, a few laughs—that's enough. But if you can't deal with that, then I guess you *don't* have anything to give me.''

Her words twisted in his gut. He ignored the sensation. "You don't mean that, Katie. It sounds good, but it's not you.''

She made a strangled sound of frustration. "When are you going to get it, Michael? I'm not your dorky little friend anymore. I'm not shy and naïve and gullible. I don't need to be protected. I'm not even a virgin— but then *you* should know that.''

The brush of flannel against his flesh... Katie beneath him, his mouth muffling her cry of pain... Michael caught his breath at the image. "The other night... I didn't think... you weren't—''

"A virgin?'' she interrupted, lifting her chin, torn between flinging the truth at him and saving her pride. "Why would it matter? I'm thirty years old, Michael, hardly jailbait.''

His jaw tightened. "It would matter.''

Pride won. "No. The other night wasn't the first time.''

He looked so relieved it would have been comical had it not hurt so much. Katherine dragged her gloved hands through her hair. "You were right, we've both had enough. Enough of each other's company, enough of this mangled excuse for a friendship.'' She turned and started in the direction of the parking lot. "I'm going home."

Before she'd gone two steps he caught her elbow and spun her around. "Don't do this, Katie."

She tossed her head back. "Don't do what?"

"We're friends."

"Are we?" She laughed without humor. "Years ago we were friends. We were young and responsible for nothing but figuring out how to fill our days. We've both grown up, Michael. Eight years have brought a lot of changes. We don't need each other anymore, not the way we used to."

"Dammit, Katie."

Before she realized what he meant to do, he jerked her against his chest and pressed his mouth to hers. The kiss was quick and hard; there seemed to be an edge of despair in it, the shadow of some savage need to possess. Katherine gasped; her head fell back.

He broke the contact but his mouth still hovered only a whisper from hers. She gazed up at him, mesmerized by his dark, stormy eyes, unable to pull away even if she had wanted to. Her lips tingled; they felt bruised. She wanted more, much more. Her heart beat heavily, maddeningly, against the wall of her chest as he brought his lips to hers once more. The second meeting was as domineering, as desperate as the first; when Michael lifted his mouth, they were both panting.

He tightened his fingers, then dropped his hands. "I still think of you as my friend, Katie."

Katherine stared at him in shock. To follow those almost violent kisses with that statement was absurd. Angry color flew to her cheeks. "Why can't you admit that what we've been feeling has nothing to do with friendship and everything to do with passion? Why won't you admit you want me?'' She drew in a quick, steadying breath; the cold air stung the back of her throat. ''Are you afraid that maybe you'll realize you *do* have something to give?''

Without waiting for a response, she spun on her heel and started for the car. She had almost reached it when his voice stopped her.

''Wanting you has never been in question, Katie. I do.''

His words sounded lost against the cold, black night, and she stopped and turned back toward him. Half of his face was bathed in the light from a floodlamp, the other was drenched in darkness. The combination of shadow and form made his expression seem hard, even grim. He looked like a man with too many ghosts. She felt a twinge but pushed it away. ''Then what *is* in question, Michael?''

He started for her, his feet crunching against the dusting of salt and sand on the parking lot. ''Nothing. You made your feelings, your needs, clear. So did I.''

She realized her hands were trembling and shoved them into her pockets. ''What are you suggesting?''

He stopped in front of her. Reaching out, he trailed a finger down her cheek. ''Sex,'' he said, almost without intonation. ''Physical gratification, a few laughs between consenting adults. More than a one-night stand but less than an affair. Is that what you want, Katie? You want to have a fling? No strings, no promises, no future?''

Tears plucked at the back of her eyelids. He was offering her only a small portion of what she wanted, and even though she'd professed to want nothing more, she could back down and he wouldn't ask any questions. But wasn't that what she'd always done when it came to Michael? Wasn't that what had left her alone and wondering to begin with? She would take a shot. Either way she had nothing to lose. "Two consenting adults. No strings, no promises."

"You're sure?"

"Yes."

Without another word, Michael helped her into the car and they headed home.

Nine

The drive home seemed to pass at the speed of light and at the same time, drag interminably. Katherine realized her palms were sweating as she followed Michael into the dark condominium. They hadn't said a dozen words since leaving the parking lot, and she felt awkward and uncertain. What happened next? She cleared her throat. "Well . . ."

Michael locked the door and turned to her. He cocked his head. "Well."

She cleared her throat again. "I guess I'll turn in. I'm pretty tired."

"Pretty tired?" His gaze drifted slowly over her. "How tired is that?"

Her knees were shaking and Katherine shifted from one foot to the other. Then he started toward her, and she thought they might buckle. "Really tired," she said quickly.

"That's too bad." He stopped in front of her.

"Yes, well I—" Without warning, he gathered her into his arms and lowered his mouth to hers. His kiss was slow, deep and shattering; when he lifted his head her limbs were shaking for a different reason.

"I'll say good-night then." He dropped a light kiss on the tip of her nose. "Sleep tight, Katie."

Shocked, she watched him disappear down the hall. That was it? One kiss and 'good night'? He wasn't even going to try... he didn't want... Her cheeks grew hot as she realized she wanted him very much, wanted him so badly her whole body tingled with it.

Annoyed with herself and him, she started for her own bedroom. Once inside, she slipped out of her clothes and into her gown. Her feet were cold, and she pulled on a pair of sweat socks.

Katherine stared at her closed bedroom door, willing it to open, for Michael to come for her. As the minutes ticked by, her shoulders drooped. This was ridiculous. She wanted him and they'd agreed that they would have—she swallowed—a fling. So why was she sitting here at the edge of her bed alone?

There was absolutely no reason to be, she assured herself. She'd already made the commitment; the hard part was done. Sucking in a deep breath and squaring her shoulders, Katherine stood up. Ignoring the quivering sensation in the pit of her stomach, she crossed the room.

The trip down the hall took too few seconds, and before she lost her courage, Katherine grasped Michael's doorknob and twisted. The door swung silently open, she crossed the threshold, then stopped. He was sitting on the bed waiting for her. He was naked.

The moonlight played over his splendid body, and she drew a shuddering breath. He looked so strong, so male. Everything about her that was female trembled in response.

"How did you know I'd come?" she whispered, her voice almost unintelligibly husky, the pulse pounding in her head.

"I didn't."

"But—" she looked down at the floor, then back at him "—what if I hadn't?"

"I would have come for you."

He pushed himself up from the bed and his muscles bunched, then eased. He stood gloriously nude and unabashed before her, and Katherine couldn't tear her eyes away. She realized her palms were wet at the same instant she acknowledged there were places that were wetter. And warmer.

When she met his gaze again, he said, "I have no future to give you, Katie."

"It doesn't matter."

"You can still change your mind. It's not too late."

"Yes, it is."

He held out his hand. "Come here."

She did, stopping only when to go further would have meant pressing herself to him. She grasped the fabric of her gown and started to pull the garment over her head.

"No." He caught her hands and brought them to his lips. "Leave it."

"But it's so—" He slid his hand down her back to cup her derriere, and her quickly drawn breath caught the words. He pulled her to him and even through the flannel she could feel his arousal.

He lowered his mouth to hers, and their tongues met. Clinging to one another, they fell to the bed. Michael's body pressed her into the mattress and, as it had twelve years ago, her gown worked up over her thighs until finally Michael eased it over her head and tossed it aside.

As he slipped inside her, she clutched at him with a force that would leave marks; his mouth caught her cries of pleasure. Their lovemaking was silent and furious—more about passion and desperation than about need or tenderness.

But the edge of tenderness was there, Katherine thought later, as her breathing began to slow, her flesh cool. It always was with Michael. He said he had nothing to give her, yet when they were together like this, it seemed he gave her everything. She trailed a finger over his damp stomach. Or did she just imagine the tenderness, the sharing, because she needed to? Maybe Michael was a good lover because he made every woman feel the same. The image of the young woman in the parking lot, her body pressed to Michael's, shot into her head and Katherine shuddered and pushed the image away. She couldn't believe that. Not and maintain her sanity.

"Are you all right?" Michael nuzzled the top of her head. "Cold?"

"I'm fine."

"Regrets."

"No."

"Good." Michael ran the soft, fuzzy fabric of her gown between his fingers. "You want to hear something funny?"

She lifted her head to see his face. His lips had curved but there was no humor in his eyes or tone. "Sure."

"This makes me feel eighteen again." He lifted the flannel gown, just a little, with his forefinger. "And totally befuddled."

She rolled onto her side and propped herself on her elbow. "My nightgown? I don't understand."

"Back at school I had a dream about us making love." He drew his eyebrows together as he ran the flat of his hand over the curve of her hip. "It was so real that at first I wondered—" he laughed tightly and shook his head "—in the dream you were wearing one of these flannel gowns and sweat socks."

Katherine went stock-still, afraid if she moved she would find that *this* was only a dream. After all the time that had passed, after all the hurt, to learn that in his own way he remembered. "Oh, my God." It was all she could say, and even then her throat closed over the words.

"Tell me about it." He smiled and this time there was a trace of amusement in the expression. "I've carried that dream around with me ever since—and had a truly bizarre fascination with sweat socks and flannel." He wiggled his eyebrows at her. "Kinky, isn't it?"

Katherine's heart beat so heavily in her chest she thought it might break through. She was delighted; she was terrified. She'd held on to this secret for so long, she wasn't certain the words would even form on her tongue. Just as she wondered how Michael would react to the truth, he began again.

"I was a lot of things back then, but at least I can't claim to have been a defiler of virgins. Every woman I've ever been with has known her way around. And exactly what she was getting into." An edge crept into his voice. "No, I left that type of thing for my father."

Katherine's blood went cold as she thought of what Sam had told her about Michael, his father and mother. She couldn't tell him. Not now, maybe never. It would only affirm everyone's comments of "like father, like son," and she couldn't hurt Michael that way.

She slid her arms around his neck and met his eyes. "I'll have to go shopping tomorrow—flannel shirts, flannel slacks, flannel sheets..."

With a husky laugh, Michael lowered his head. "Don't forget sweat socks. Lots and lots of them."

The following Friday night, Katherine popped her workout tape into the VCR, then sank onto the white carpeting. It was over. Tomorrow, the study would be declared a bust, its participants set free. Michael would move out of her house and, she feared, out of her life.

Would he go back to the woman she'd seen him with in the parking lot? Katherine realized her palms were damp and wiped them against her thighs. She'd often wondered about the long-legged blonde, had wondered if he still saw her, wondered if the woman knew about her and Michael. She'd never had the guts, or the heart, to ask, and it bothered her that she might be one of those women who would ignore rather than face the truth.

Even wondering about it now brought an ache so sharp that for a moment, Katherine couldn't breathe. She sucked in air, trying to reason with herself. This week Michael wouldn't have had the time, or the energy, to see another woman. The days had flown by in a whirlwind of passion and passion's lethargy. It seemed that she and Michael had spent more time in bed than out of it. They'd even eaten in bed—finger-food feasts that Michael had brought home expressly for that purpose.

Katherine sighed and flopped back against the thick, white pile. When they were making love, she felt wonderful, and when they weren't, she was depressed. Depressed because Michael didn't love her and because nothing could change that fact—no amount of wishing, praying or cajoling. Right now, their "affair" was convenient. When it was no longer easy, and without love, the passion would burn out, without love. Besides, she knew—without proof, but in her gut—that Michael wasn't happy.

Katherine frowned and plucked at the carpeting, ignoring the perky aerobic instructor on the screen. Why did she think that? He'd been attentive, passionate, romantic—the kind of lover most women only dreamed about. He never tired of her, and . . .

And it seemed that theirs, the most intimate of relationships, lacked intimacy. Katherine scowled up at the ceiling. Now, that was nonsense.

Her chest tightened, and she squeezed her eyes shut. It wasn't. Michael was holding a part of himself from her—an essential part, the part that really made two people lovers. The part he had never held from her before.

She wanted to scoff at her own thoughts again, but she wasn't even up to the charade. The truth was, she and Michael hadn't talked all week. Oh, they'd teased and made love-talk, but all in all they'd shared nothing more than the moment and their bodies.

Maybe she just needed the three magic words to make her happy. Maybe she was too greedy, selfish, inexperienced. Katherine shook her head. No, it wasn't any of those things. It was the hopelessness of their relationship; it was the fact that Michael always talked in terms of goodbye.

But still, Katherine thought resolutely, other women would kill for what she— She curled her fingers into her palms in frustration. She wasn't other women; it wasn't enough.

"You're not going to stay in shape that way."

Katherine's eyes snapped open. Michael was standing over her, smiling wickedly. She looked from him to the workout in progress on the television screen and blushed. "I guess I didn't feel like exercising tonight."

He made a great show of disappointment and squatted down next to her. "Not at all?" He ran a finger over the creamy triangle of flesh exposed by the leotard's deep V. "Maybe I could change your mind."

Her heart started rapping against her chest. He'd only been home a couple of moments and it had started already—they were being glib and sexual and superficial. But she hadn't the strength of will to stop and found her lips curving despite a lingering sense of sadness. "I'm awfully tired."

"Are you sure—" he dipped the finger underneath the stretchy fabric and the peaks of her breasts tightened with excitement "—I couldn't do anything to convince you?"

Katherine sighed as his hand moved lower; her eyes fluttered shut. "I suppose if you worked...very hard."

Michael laughed softly and removed his hand. "Speaking of..." He straightened her leotard and stood back up. "This will have to wait, my sexy professor, because I have work to do."

Katherine pouted—she couldn't help herself. "You have to go in to the bar tonight?"

"Nope. I have work to do right here."

"Here?" She sat up and watched as he retrieved a metal toolbox and a large shopping bag. "What's that?"

"A surprise." His eyes crinkled at the corners. "Go back to your workout."

Frowning, she jumped up and followed him to the kitchen. He looked entirely too pleased with himself. "I thought we'd already established that I didn't want to exercise." Her frown deepened as he took a hammer and screwdriver out of the toolbox. What was he going to do with those? "Michael, I don't like surprises."

"Spoilsport." Whistling, he opened the window over the sink and proceeded to unfasten the screen. Cold air barreled in from outside.

Goose bumps rose on her bare arms, and Katherine hugged herself. "Michael, you do know that it's fr—"

"I know." He smiled and carefully levered the screen through the window and inside. "Look in the bag and die, Katie."

She stopped in her tracks. The man must have eyes in the back of his head, she thought, sniffing. "Okay, go ahead and destroy my house, leap if you want. Since you seem intent on freezing us, I'm going to put on some warm clothes."

"Great." His smile widened. "And don't come back for twenty minutes."

Nineteen-and-a-half minutes later Katherine pushed open the kitchen door and stepped cautiously inside. Michael was making a pot of hot chocolate—it was unbearably cold in the room—and grinning like a satisfied cat.

She moved her eyes from him to the window; her mouth dropped. He'd hung a bird feeder outside her kitchen window. It was designed to look like a Swiss chalet; it hung off a bracket that was attached to the window frame. And by the looks of the bright red cardinal perched there and pecking away, he'd already filled it.

Pulse fluttering, Katherine crossed to the window. The cardinal paused and looked at her, then as if understanding there was a barrier between them, continued to enjoy his meal.

Katherine turned slowly back to Michael, blinking against the tears in her eyes. "I don't know what to say. This is so sweet...I..." Her throat closed over the words, and she turned back to the window. A little brown sparrow had joined the cardinal, and the two birds had formed an uneasy alliance.

Michael came up behind her. He wrapped his arms around her and nestled her back against his chest, resting his chin on the top of her head. "I wanted you to have some company...after I leave."

The pain in her chest made her breathless. She squeezed her eyes shut, and when she reopened them, the cardinal was gone. "Thank you. I love...it."

Michael seemed not to notice the awkwardness of her last words. He rubbed his cheek against her hair. "Susi was in this morning."

Katherine blinked at the sudden change in subject and turned herself around in his arms. He hadn't mentioned Susi since before the party. "She was?"

"Uh-huh." A teasing light was back in Michael's eyes. "She brought a gift."

"She did?" There was no reason why she should be jealous, Katherine scolded herself. Michael wasn't interested in Susi except as the daughter of an old friend. She was jealous anyway.

"Yup." Michael pressed a kiss onto her forehead, then released her. "Chocolate?" He didn't wait for an answer, just started filling two mugs with the steaming beverage.

"What was it?"

He handed her a cup. "An Icelandic wool sweater."

"Oh?" She angled her chin up, just a little. "Why aren't you wearing it?"

"It wasn't for me."

It took several seconds for his words to register. When they did, her eyes widened, then narrowed. "If not for you, then who?"

Michael smiled. "Seems she came looking for me one evening when I wasn't in and ended up talking to Tommy, my new bartender. My new *college-age* bartender. One thing led to another, and now I'm out of the picture."

Katherine's heart sank. The only reason she'd been able to come up with that he might want to continue living with her—Susi—was no longer a viable one. "How convenient," she said, forcing nonchalance. "Now you're really off the hook."

"What do you mean?"

"The study." Katherine looked at him over the rim of her cup. "It's been cancelled. I found out this morning; Marilyn will officially announce it to you tomorrow." Something flashed in his eyes, then was gone so quickly she thought she'd imagined it.

"I see." He brought his drink to his lips. "So, I have one more interview?"

"Yes."

"What were the results?"

"Overwhelmingly negative. Marilyn's discouraged."

"Too bad. How's the chocolate?"

"Fine." Katherine glanced down at her untouched drink. He hadn't reacted at all to her news, she thought miserably. But why should she have hoped differently? He'd been honest and had given her just what he promised—physical gratification with no strings and no future. Tears welled in her eyes, and she turned back to the bird feeder. She wanted to ask what it was going to mean in terms of their affair—fling, she corrected herself—but this time, even calling herself a coward didn't help. She kept her mouth shut.

The next morning Michael slammed his car door behind him and started across the parking lot in front of the Social Sciences building. The day was brilliant but cold. March, one of the most unpredictable months in Rockford, was living up to its reputation. Yesterday the temperature had skyrocketed to the sixties, but overnight a cold front had come through and it had plummeted to freezing again.

Michael scowled and pulled his collar up around his neck. His foul mood had nothing to do with the weather and everything to do with Katherine and his own feelings.

The truth was, he felt too much. He'd even been foolish enough to toy with the idea that maybe, just maybe, there could be a chance for him. He glared up at the clear blue sky. Dammit, he shouldn't have gotten himself into this situation in the first place. He'd known all along what kind of man he was; he should have let her walk away. It would have been better for them both.

But he hadn't been able to do that. Being with her had felt too good, and he'd wanted her in a way he'd never wanted a woman before. She'd become an obsession. So he'd tried a compromise—a physical relationship, one where the guidelines and limitations were clearly delineated at the start. He'd presented it as bluntly as possible, hoping she would back off—and praying she wouldn't.

In the same paradoxical vein, the past week had been heaven...and hell. When he was with her, he felt stirrings he thought had long ago died inside him and started to believe in things he'd given up on years ago. But every time he began to believe and feel, he would think about all the reasons why he shouldn't.

Michael climbed the building's steps, swung open one of the doors and went inside. He stopped, unzipped his coat and pulled off his gloves, drawing his eyebrows together. He'd been twelve the first time he'd angrily confronted his father. He remembered demanding, *Mom loves you. How could you have treated her that way?* Just as clearly, he remembered being stunned by his father's answer. *I loved your mother, but I can't change who I am.*

Michael dragged a hand through his hair; it was crisp and cold against his fingers. The study ending would be the perfect opportunity to end their affair. He could slip gradually out of Katherine's life, seeing her less and less until both had forgotten what they'd shared.

There was an unfamiliar ache in his chest, and Michael drew in a slow breath. It didn't ease the pain, so he absently rubbed the spot over his heart. Maybe she wouldn't have trouble forgetting, but he would. His obsession with her hadn't lessened as he'd hoped it would; instead, obsession had become necessity, and he didn't know if he could let her go. And that was dangerous.

He stopped in front of Marilyn's office. The door was open; she was at her desk surrounded by disordered stacks of paper. "Hi, Marilyn. You ready for me?"

The redhead looked up and smiled wearily. "Come on in, Michael."

He crossed the room and slid into the chair opposite her. "I hear we won't be seeing each other again."

"Nope. This is it." She sighed and looked down at her hands. "I'm sure you also heard that the whole thing was a bust."

"Yeah. Too bad."

"I feel like a real jerk. This hypothesis started with me. And it's the first one in five years that's been a total failure. Maybe I'm not cut out to be a sociologist."

Michael grinned at her melodramatic sigh. "Better not let Dr. Reed hear you say that. She'll feel obligated to give you one of her inspirational talks."

Marilyn smiled warmly. "She's quite the little cheerleader, isn't she?"

"She always has been. It's one of the things . . ." He saw Marilyn's speculative glance and cleared his throat. "So, what kind of probing, too-personal questions are you going to ask me today?"

"None. Today you fill out—" She started shuffling through the papers in front of her, huffing when after several moments she still hadn't found what she was looking for.

"You know, Marilyn, I'm not the most organized person, but—"

"No comments from the peanut gallery. Ah—" she pulled a manila file folder out of one of the stacks; as she did several others slid to the floor "—here it is. As I was saying, today you fill out another questionnaire.

This one is similar to the one you were given when the study began. However, the questions are subtly—"

"Excuse me." They both turned to the doorway. Ron was there and looked flustered. "Marilyn, I need a little help over here. Tracy Lynn's—"

"Oh, no."

"Oh, yes. She's hysterical about the study ending. Says she can't live without Nick."

"The soap opera continues," Marilyn muttered, jumping up. "Michael, the questionnaire is right on top, so go ahead and start filling it in. I'll be back as soon as I can."

Bemused Michael watched her go, then turned back toward the desk. He shook his head as he reached for the file folder on top. As promised, the questionnaire was right in front. He took it out, then, unable to help himself, started leafing through the rest of the file's contents.

All his comments were there, as were Marilyn's evaluation of them.

No indication of any change...seems unaffected by cohabitation...uncommunicative this week... totally indifferent—too indifferent?

Michael raised his eyebrows as he went on. Marilyn was good. He'd done his best to be evasive, but she'd still suspected something was going on between him and Katherine. Of course, maybe Katherine had said something...

His lips curved wickedly. He shouldn't. Katherine would be furious if she ever found out...Marilyn could walk back in at any moment... He saw Katherine's name peeking out from beneath several other folders and shot a quick glance at the door. Well, he'd never claimed to be a Boy Scout.

He pulled the file out of the pile, taking care not to disturb any others, and flipped it open. He frowned. It was practically empty. There was the original questionnaire and the responses from the interview they'd attended together and nothing else. Scrawled across the top of the questionnaire in red was *disqualified*. Disqualified? What in—

"Whew! Am I glad that's over with. How's everything going in—what are you doing?"

Michael looked up at Marilyn, his heart thumping uncomfortably in his chest. "What is this?" He held up the piece of paper. "Why was Katherine disqualified from the experiment?"

Marilyn snatched the questionnaire from his hands, her cheeks growing pink. "How dare you—"

"I asked you a question."

Marilyn stuffed the paper back into the file. "Maybe you better ask Dr. Reed."

"I'm asking you."

"It's not my information to share," she said uncomfortably, shifting her gaze.

He stood and faced her. She still wouldn't meet his eyes and there was a sinking sensation in the pit of his stomach. "This has something to do with me, doesn't it?"

She met his eyes then. "Michael, please...talk to Katherine."

"I will." He grabbed his coat and strode from the office.

Michael made the drive home in record time. His heart beating a staccato rhythm, he softly closed the front door behind him and went in search of Katherine.

He found her in the kitchen. She was humming as she read the paper. He stared at her. Her head was tipped down and her inky hair spilled across her face, concealing her expression. He thought of how the strands felt against his fingers and lowered his eyes. She was still in her robe and the loose flaps revealed the beginning of one creamy breast. His stomach tightened. What would he do without her?

"Katie?"

She looked up in surprise, with a welcoming smile. "You're home early. I'm not even..." Her smile faded. "Is something wrong?"

"Why were you disqualified from the study?"

Her fingers curled around the newspaper, crumpling it. "What do you mean?"

He set his jaw. "Give it up, Katie. You haven't participated since the second week. Why?"

"How did you find out?"

"It doesn't matter."

She carefully folded the newspaper, then dropped her hands to her lap. They were trembling, and she laced her fingers together. "I had to withdraw from the study because I was prejudiced from the first. If I had remained an active participant, my responses would have contaminated the final results."

"Why?" When she only stared at him, he tore off his gloves, tossed them on the counter, then ran a hand through his hair. "If I remember the prerequisites," he said slowly, his eyes locked with hers, "to participate you couldn't have previously cohabitated with a member of the opposite sex, either in or outside marriage, and you couldn't have had a relationship, a sexual...relationship...with your..." He read it in her eyes and it was like a fist to his chest. "Tell me it's not true, Katie."

"I'm sorry. I can't do that."

"Oh, God." He strode to the window and looked out at the empty bird feeder. When he felt he could speak again, he turned back to her. "The dream?" She nodded and he stared at her in shock, all the bits and snatches of memories coming together. The night Sheila had dumped him, he'd gone to Katherine. He'd been drunk and hurting. As he'd known she would, Katherine had held him and comforted him, then helped him to his room. She'd tried to guide him to his bed, but they'd lost their balance and had tumbled to the mattress... The image filled his head and Michael looked down at his hands, remembering what he'd said to her, how he'd coaxed and complimented.

The memory, the truth, left a vile taste in his mouth. It hadn't been a dream. Drunk, he had lured his best friend into bed, taken her virginity, then fallen asleep without even holding and comforting her. Without cherishing her. He was no better than his father. Worse.

"That night ... you didn't get—" he had to force the words out "—pregnant did you?"

"No." she prayed she didn't sound as shaken as she felt. She knew, somehow, that for her to be calm and together was important. It might be her only chance.

He met her eyes. "Why didn't you tell me what happened? Then or since? I gave you the perfect opportunity the other night. Why didn't you use it?"

The blood pounded in her head. "I was young...uncertain of myself. Your memory lapse seemed a convenient way out of an embarrassing situation. After that, I just wanted to forget..." At his anguished expression, her heart stopped, for just a moment, before recovering its wild pace again. She drew in a deep, steadying breath, choosing her words carefully. "The other night, I suspected how you'd react, knew it would hurt you. I decided to leave the past where it belonged."

"Nice sentiment," he said, his voice harsh. "But the past has a way of creeping up on you."

"It doesn't have to."

He ignored the comment and emitted a bark of laughter. "What really kills me is, after how I hurt you, you're worried about my feelings. I deserve your anger, your disdain." He balled his hands into fists. "You were my best friend. You helped me, trusted me . . . believed I was better than my reputation. How did I repay you? I took you to bed, took your virginity, then fell asleep. God, I didn't even remember it afterward! How you must have felt!"

Katherine felt the stirrings of anger and stood and crossed to him. Facing him, she forced him to look at her. "What's all this 'took,' Michael? I went willingly to bed with you, I *gave* you my virginity. I wanted it to happen."

"You wanted more than a one-night stand," he said brutally. "More than a quickie with a drunk."

She couldn't lie, although she knew it would be best to. "Yes, I wanted more. But that doesn't release me from all responsibility. I should have told you that; I should have been honest. Instead I pretended and hid and played games. Not much has changed in eight years—an hour ago I was still evading and pretending."

"And now?" He reached up and touched her cheek. Her skin was like satin against his fingertips and he willed himself to remember the sensation long after he knew she would have forgotten his face.

"Now I'm tired—of playing games, of pretending, of dodging my own feelings." She took a deep breath. "I love you, Michael. I always have."

"But . . . when we started this . . . affair, you told me it was just for laughs. You told me—"

"I lied."

Panic threaded through him. Panic and something else. Something that made him breathless and aching. "We have no future."

She covered his hand with her own and held his gaze. "We could." She saw the denial in his expression, felt it in the way he seemed to withdraw from her. Honesty hadn't made a bit of difference. He'd already made his decision. She whirled away from him. Without turning, she asked, "What are you so afraid of? I asked you that the other night; you never answered."

"I care about you, but I know who I am, Katie. I'm not the marrying kind."

Angry color rose to her cheeks, and she looked over her shoulder at him. "So if I'd continued to pretend this was just for laughs, everything would be fine? Meaningless sex is okay, but love and commitment are dirty words?"

Denial jumped to his lips; he swallowed it. What they'd shared had been far from meaningless . . . but he couldn't tell her because he couldn't allow her to hope. Instead, he shrugged and said, "We both knew what we were getting into. We talked about it, Katie. I can't help it that you lied." He started for the door, knowing he'd lied, too. "I'm going to pack."

She stared at the empty doorway, the pain in her chest almost unbearable. She was going to lose him. After all this time, after everything they'd been through. Tears flooded her eyes, and she blinked. It was crazy. She knew in her heart that he felt something for her, something more than friendship, something strong enough to scare him into leaving.

Taking a deep breath, she swiped at the moisture on her cheeks. She wasn't giving up! Not yet, not when there might be a chance. Squaring her shoulders, she flew down the hallway.

He was emptying his bureau drawers into a suitcase. It took all her control not to cry out. "You still haven't answered me, Michael. What are you afraid of? The future—or the past?" His hands stilled, just for a moment, and she knew the truth. Suddenly everything made sense—his refusal to face his feelings, to let her close, to commit. "That's it, isn't it? You're so afraid of the past, so terrified of finding out the truth about yourself once and for all that you're willing to throw away the future."

"Save yourself the aggravation, Katie. The Tardo men aren't known for their dependability."

She crossed the room and grabbed his arm, forcing him to look at her. "You're not your father, Michael." She could imagine a six-year-old boy, trying to deal with his own grief as well as his mother's. She could see him as a young man dealing with the guilt and fear created by a remarkable resemblance to the man who had hurt them both. She thought of Sam's words. "And I'm not your mother. We're not them."

"No?" He turned her so they both faced into the mirror. "Don't the similarities strike you? Don't you wonder if, through us, history is being repeated? Don't you think you should be running away from me as far and as fast as you can?"

Uncomfortable, she tore her gaze from the image in the mirror. "I won't deny the parallels. But they don't mean a thing, Michael. Coincidence." She cupped his face in her palms. "History doesn't have to be repeated. It can be changed. I learned that . . . I changed it."

"There's one more similarity, Katie," he said, his tone deliberately harsh, knowing it was the only way. "My father didn't love my mother . . . and I don't love you."

Katherine jerked away from him as if he'd slapped her. Tears sprang to her eyes, threatening to overflow. She thought she'd known pain before—she'd been wrong. Gathering every scrap of control and pride she possessed, she looked him full in the face. "I see," she said, her voice small and tight.

The wounded look in her eyes ripped at him, and it took everything Michael had not to pull her into his arms. She was better off without him. Chest aching, he snapped his suitcase shut. He crossed to the door, then stopped and looked over his shoulder at her. "This is for the best, Katherine. Someday you'll see that."

Ten

Michael stared at the clock above the bar. In one hour the group from the study would be meeting to present the tabulated responses and tie up any loose ends. He'd gotten the call from Marilyn a couple of days ago.

Hearing the other woman's voice had made him think of Katherine. Michael groaned and plucked a cocktail straw from the box. Of course, everything made him think of Katherine. And every time he thought of her, he hurt.

Michael squeezed his fingers around the straw, the edges biting into his hand. He loved her; he had for a long time. He'd realized the truth at the same moment he'd denied it to her. Flinging the mangled straw in the trash, he cursed under his breath. What ripped him apart was, it didn't change a thing. She was still smart and sweet and perfect, and he was still the type of man who would walk out on a sleeping woman.

He checked the clock again. Fifty-two minutes. He wanted to see her, wanted so badly the need gnawed at him. But he couldn't bear to see her and not hold her. His lips curved in self-derision. Not that she would let him within three feet of her. The look in her eyes when he'd walked out had made that clear enough. It was over.

At the tightening in his chest, Michael swore again. Wasn't that what he'd tried to do? Hadn't his intention been to make her forget him, to turn her against him so she could go on to someone who would give her a good, happy life? It was for the best. Really it was.

He dragged both hands through his hair. If that was true, why hadn't he been able to sleep, eat or work? And why did it feel as if his heart had been wrenched from his body?

"Pour me a whiskey, boy! I'm parched."

Michael jerked his head up, smiling for the first time in days. Sam Steele was just inside the door, his arms loaded with bags from a burger joint known for their half-pound patties. "Sam, why do I have the feeling Lily thinks you're at the office eating the healthy lunch she fixed you this morning?"

"Sprouts," Sam grumbled, crossing the room. "A man needs meat, something that'll stick to his ribs." He dumped the bags on the bar, then shrugged out of his coat and sat down. "What the wife doesn't know won't hurt her. Where's that whiskey?"

Michael drew him a light beer, then laughed at the look his friend sent him. "What can I say? Lily's got me on the payroll."

"It's a conspiracy," Sam mumbled, taking a long swallow. After another swallow and a discreet belch, he narrowed his eyes on Michael. "You look like hell, boy. What's up?"

Michael thought of Katherine, and his smile faded. "Nothing I want to talk about."

"Humph. You told me the same thing at sixteen when I caught you siphoning gas from my truck." Sam pushed his empty mug toward Michael. "This wouldn't have anything to do with that little gal you're in love with?" When Michael shot him a sharp glance, he laughed. "I knew the way things were between you two the moment I saw you together at the party. You've got it about as bad as a man can."

The party. In agonizing detail Michael remembered the way Katherine had melted in his arms, fitting to him as if her body had been fashioned for his, and he ached for her. "You know, Sam, Lily told me last week that she suspected you were sneaking beef. I told her I doubted it, but at the time I didn't—"

Sam held up his hands. "What? Blackmail again! To think I lent you money! To think I—"

"Stow it, Steele. Our burgers are getting cold."

As they ate they talked about sports, the bar business and Sam's store. When the last of the burgers and fries had been consumed, Michael sent the other man an assessing glance. He'd never been able to hide the truth from Sam, but by the same token, he could read his old friend pretty well himself. Something was up. He decided to find out what it was.

"This is more than a social call, Sam. Care to fill me in?"

The older man pulled a cigar out of his vest pocket, nipped the end, then lit it. He leaned back, puffing on the stogie for several moments, watching Michael through the cloud of smoke. Finally he said, "I've been thinking about your father a lot lately."

Michael's hands stilled on the take-out bags, then he crushed them and tossed them in the trash. "Funny, so have I. But I have to, what's your excuse?"

"Something your Katherine said." Sam looked from the end of his cigar to Michael. "He was a real S.O.B."

"Just figure that out?"

"Nope, knew it from the first. But I never told you how I felt."

"Some things aren't necessary."

"Maybe, maybe not." Sam contemplated the glowing tip again. "I always thought you knew how proud I was of you, how tickled I was with the way you've turned out. Now I'm not so sure."

Michael scowled, uncomfortable. "What's this leading up to?"

"I called the house looking for you. Katherine told me you moved out."

He'd talked to Katherine. Longing, so poignant it took his breath away, rushed through him. A dozen questions jumped to his lips; Michael reminded himself she was out of his life and swallowed them. Lifting his soft drink to his lips, he shrugged. "Is that so?"

"Yes, dammit!" Sam slammed his palm against the bar. "And she sounded like you look—brokenhearted." When Michael didn't comment, his cheeks reddened. "What's wrong with you, boy? You can't throw a woman like that away! You can't—"

"Sam," Michael warned, "you don't know anything about me and Katherine. Drop it."

"I know this—" he waved the cigar in Michael's face "—only a fool would throw away love."

Michael clenched his fists. "Love doesn't change anything," he said, his voice hard. "It doesn't change who I am or what I'm capable of. Let me tell you a little story. When Katherine and I were in school together, we were friends. The best of friends. One night I went to her room drunk, coaxed her into bed and took her virginity. I didn't even remember what had happened the next day. Pretty picture, huh?" His jaw tightened. "And here's the kicker, Sam. I loved her. I'm the kind of man who treats the woman he loves like—"

"You were young."

"So was my father," Michael shot back. "And like you said, he was a real S.O.B.—"

"Your father never loved anyone but himself," Sam interrupted, stamping out his cigar. "He was selfish, self-centered and immature. And whatever he told you, forget it. He was also a liar. That man would say anything to get what he wanted, or to get himself out of Dutch."

Michael stared at him, stunned silent. He'd never seen his old friend this way. Sam was good-naturedly gruff, rough around the edges but easygoing. Even when he'd caught him siphoning gas out of his truck, he hadn't lost his temper, not really. But now... now his face was flushed with anger and a vein throbbed in his neck.

"And your mother's a lot of things, Michael, but strong isn't one of them. Instead of focusing on herself and how she'd been hurt, she should have spent a little more time worrying about her son. We all should have. Instead of making comparisons based on looks, we should have—"

"I was fine."

"My butt. You were a little kid and you were scared."

There was a strange sensation in the pit of Michael's stomach. Trying to ignore it, he looked Sam dead in the eye. "Why are you telling me this?"

"You're a smart boy, figure it out." The older man slid off the bar stool and pulled on his coat. That done, he looked back at Michael. "The other night, I was looking for you because I wanted to thank you."

Michael shoved his hands into his pockets. "What for?"

"For not being your father's son. That's right," he added at Michael's scoff. "My daughter doesn't use the good sense God gave her. Your father wouldn't have thought twice about taking her up on her offer."

Michael drew his eyebrows together, watching as Sam crossed the room. When he reached the door he stopped and glanced back over his shoulder. "Ponder that before you throw it all away, Michael." Then he was gone.

Michael stared at the empty doorway, the unsettling sensation in his stomach spreading. He'd never considered that his father could have lied to him about loving his mother or about the reason he left. And he'd bought into everything his father had told him because he'd been young and scared and desperate to hear that his father wasn't such a bad guy.

I loved your mother, but I can't change who I am. Michael grimaced as his father's words rang in his ears. With that statement—lie, he corrected—his father had freed himself from all responsibility. And that was the difference between himself and his father—he'd taken responsibility for who he'd *thought* he was all along.

Michael looked down at his hands. Sam was right. Although Susi was gorgeous, taking her up on her offer had never even crossed his mind. He hadn't wanted to hurt her...just as he hadn't wanted to hurt Katie. His own feelings, needs, had taken a back seat to those of others.

His father had never worried about anyone but himself. Michael's lips curved into a smile, the smile led to a burst of laughter. He wasn't like his father. Maybe he had been once, but not anymore. He'd made his choice years ago—to care about other people, to be kind . . . to love and be loved.

Katie. He had to see her, had to tell her what he'd learned and how he felt. Shouting for his waitress to take care of everything until his relief came in, he grabbed his jacket and headed out the door.

Katherine stepped out of her car, her lips tilting into a smile. The day was wet but warm; in the distance she could hear bird song. It was hard to believe that spring might actually be here. She pushed the hair away from her face, her smile vanishing. The way she felt inside, it might never be spring again.

She reached back into the car for her briefcase, then slammed the door shut behind her and started across the parking lot. The three weeks since Michael had walked out of her life had passed slowly, second by second, minute by minute. But they had passed. And in that time the pain had deadened, but not eased. If that made any sense, Katherine thought, looking up at the gray sky.

She climbed the steps to the Social Sciences building and went inside. She stopped, glancing uncertainly down the hall. Would Michael be here? She thought not, but a lingering doubt—or was it hope—plucked at her. Katherine lifted her chin. Either way, it made no difference to her. He was right, she was better off without him.

Katherine's knees were trembling, just a little, and she drew in a deep breath. She was such a fake. Nothing had ever mattered to her more and she wasn't better off without him—she was miserable. And even after he had looked her in the eye and told her he didn't love her, she couldn't accept it.

She started slowly down the hall, tears flooding her eyes. She blinked, feeling like an idiot. He couldn't have been more plain or more blunt—and here she was, still hoping, still fooling herself. After eight years, nothing had changed. Maybe Michael was right, history would be repeated no matter how hard you tried to change it.

Katherine squared her shoulders. That wasn't true. She *had* changed history. The ending might have remained the same, but she'd taken a stand, she'd shaped events rather than being a pawn to them. And she would go on. She would never forget Michael, probably never stop loving him, but she would make a life for herself.

And maybe someday it wouldn't feel as if she was being torn apart, heart first.

Katherine stepped into the classroom, her eyes immediately finding Marilyn. The woman gave a small shake of her head, and a combination of disappointment and relief flooded through her. Michael hadn't come.

She silently mouthed "thank-you," then let her gaze circle the room. Contrasting sharply with the meeting eight weeks ago, there was little discussion and no laughter today; the students were gathered in small, solemn groups or sitting alone at desks, doodling or staring into space.

Katherine remembered her own first attempts at research and her first failure and tossed a reassuring smile at Marilyn. It was time for her to forget her own disappointment and deal with theirs. She snapped the door shut behind her. "Good afternoon, everybody. Are we ready to begin?"

Michael checked his watch and gunned the engine. The powerful car shot forward, making it through the light at the entrance to the college just as it turned red.

It was Friday afternoon and the campus was almost deserted. With nothing to slow him down, he angled across the parking lot, screeching to a stop at the base of the steps in front of Katherine's building. He flung open the door, intending to leave the car where it was, not caring what size ticket he got. He had to get to her, had to see her. He squeezed his eyes shut. God, please let it not be too late.

Heart pounding, he jumped out of the car and raced up the stairs. He felt freedom, maybe for the first time in his life. But with the freedom came real fear—that he'd blown it, that he really had thrown it all away.

He slammed through the doors and started down the hall at a dead run. He heard her voice and the blood rushed to his head. He'd never known a sound could be so welcome—like coming home.

He stopped outside the classroom door. She was standing in front of the group, her hands shoved into the pockets of a brown tweed blazer. Her hair was pulled back into a severe bun; she was wearing the heavy glasses he remembered from years ago. She'd never looked more beautiful.

Feeling uncertain, even vulnerable, he stepped through the door.

"—and finally, I commend you on your professional, scholarly approach. Because of your professionalism, the data you have accumulated will be of great value to future sociologists. Research isn't about being right; it's about answering questions. You did that. Congratulations." She beamed at her students. "If no one has anything to add—"

"I do," Michael said.

Katherine jerked around in surprise. Michael was standing in the doorway, his mouth curved into one of his award-winning smiles, looking happier than she'd ever seen him. She curled her fingers into her palms so tightly her nails bit into the flesh. She wasn't a woman who condoned violence, but at this moment she could have killed him. And if he didn't stop looking at her as if nothing had changed between them, she would.

"I wanted to say goodbye...and invite you all to a wedding. I hope to be getting married soon and would be pleased if—"

Katherine gripped the edge of the podium. Married? The image that had haunted her for weeks—the long-legged blonde, pressed against Michael, his head bent to look into her eyes—shot into her head. And with the image came pain, a debilitating pain that left her breathless.

He'd lied to her—about not being the marrying kind, about not being able to commit. The truth was, he'd simply left her for another woman. Blinded by tears, she gathered up her papers and shoved them into her briefcase. She darted a glance back at Michael—he'd been surrounded by students who were slapping him on the back and wishing him well. She slipped past the crowd and out into the hall. She hadn't gone a dozen steps when she heard him behind her.

"Katherine wait!"

She speeded up, pulling out the keys to her office as she did. Just before she reached the safety of her door, he caught her elbow. She jerked away from his grasp. "Don't touch me!"

Michael dropped his hand, shocked by the depth of her fury. He'd handled this all wrong. How could he have been so stupid to assume...to think... He shook his head. Talking to people, especially women, had always been easy. The right question, the perfect response, had always been on the tip of his tongue. He'd been able to soothe, woo and cajole without a second thought. But now, when it mattered, he'd totally blown it.

He saw her hands were trembling as she unlocked her office. "Katie," he said softly as she opened the door. "We need to talk."

She didn't look at him. "We said our goodbyes, Michael."

As she slipped inside, he put a hand on the door, preventing her from shutting him out. "Katie...about the engagement—"

She whirled on him then, unable to contain her anger another second. "I can't believe you came here! I can't believe—'' She brought a shaking hand to her lips, trying to compose herself. When she once again felt she could speak without completely falling apart, she asked, "Why did you pick her? Because she *doesn't* really care for you and you *don't* love her? Because that way it's nice, easy…safe?" She balled her hands into fists. "Does she know about us? Have you told her we were sleeping together?"

Michael stared at her in confusion. Who and what was she talking about? He reached out to touch her and once again she jerked away from him. "Maybe we'd better back up," he said as quietly and with as much control as he could. "I don't know what—"

"Back up?" Color flooded her cheeks and she jutted out her chin. "Isn't that too much like repeating history? You were right, Michael. You're no good for me and I'm running as fast and far as I can from you."

The sarcasm in her voice ripped at him as much as the words. He pulled her into his arms. "If you'd let me explain, Katherine. I love—"

She fought against him. "You wouldn't know love if it hit you in the face! You're so wrapped up in the past that—"

He caught her words with his mouth. He heard her quick intake of breath, felt her hands flatten and press against his chest. When he lifted his mouth she was still stiff in his arms, but at least now she was so mad she couldn't speak. It was his turn. "Yes, I would," he murmured. "And it *did* hit me right in the face. I'm still reeling from it. I love you, Katherine."

Her glasses had slipped down her nose and she tipped her head back so she could see his face. She drew her eyebrows together. "You don't love me. You love the blonde."

Michael laughed and nudged the glasses back up her nose. It wasn't like Katie to be irrational. He would take it as a good sign. "What blonde?"

"The one from the parking lot. The one you—" it still hurt and she caught her breath "—went to the morning after we made love."

"I don't know what..." His words trailed off as comprehension dawned. "You mean Susi?"

"No, not Susi. The woman who..." Her words trailed off and hope sprang to life inside her. She tried to check it. "Susi?"

"Uh-huh." Michael tightened his arms around her. "That morning she came to the condo. Apparently, she didn't believe we were living together. The clothes strewn all over the living room were pretty convincing. I walked her out to her car."

Katherine's cheeks heated. "But when I saw you, she had her hands on your shoulders and was—"

"Saying goodbye," Michael said simply. "Giving it one last try."

"Oh." Katherine rested her forehead against his chest, assimilating what he'd said. "I feel pretty dumb."

"You?" he teased. "A Ph.D.? A full professor? A—"

"Yes," she said, laughing up at him, the hope of moments before blossoming, filling her with light and warmth. She remembered then the reason he had left, and as quickly as it had blossomed, the hope withered and died. She moved out of his arms. "I don't think I can fight your ghosts, Michael. I know I can't fight the past."

"You don't have to, Katie." He reached out and touched her hair, just once, then dropped his hand. "I realized today that *I* could change history—that I already had. I realized that a person can make himself anything he wants to be, that who you are has more to do with determination and will than with blood." One corner of his mouth lifted. "I was so blinded by the past that I couldn't see the lessons I'd already learned."

"Oh, Michael." She wrapped her arms around him. "I'm happy for you."

He smiled. "Your lectures helped. So did having to do without you." He inched her glasses back up to the bridge of her nose again. "You see, even back then I loved you. I was just too young and scared to acknowledge it. All of a sudden you were out of my life, and I was devastated."

He'd loved her all along. Suddenly it seemed as if a part of her that had been torn wide open years ago was now mended. And it felt wonderful. Wonderful and warm and . . . She looked up at him then, the wonder joined by fear. "We almost lost each other," she whispered. "We could have gone our separate ways and—"

"We didn't." He caught her bottom lip between his teeth and gently tugged. "Now I'm only worried about one thing."

"One?" She looked up at him, concerned.

"Mmm, just one." He found the pulse behind her ear and pressed his lips to the spot, liking the way it throbbed in response. "I don't think I can wait till we get home to make love."

"Oh . . ." Relief flowed through her and she relaxed against him. Looping her arms around his neck, she murmured, "We could always—" she brushed her lips along his jaw "—just—" she caught an earlobe between her teeth and nipped "—stay here." She reached behind her and locked the door, then wound her fingers in his hair and pulled his head to hers. Their lips met and parted, their tongues toyed, then twined.

For long minutes they just kissed, reveling in the taste of love, the flavor of commitment. Then Katherine pushed his sweater over his head, delighting in the feel of his firm, muscled flesh under her palms and the knowledge that there was no rush—he would be with her forever.

Michael followed her lead, gently slipping her glasses off, then disposing of her soft, knit turtleneck and wool slacks. He savored the sensation of her skin against his, finding a special pleasure—pleasure that warmed not only his flesh but his whole being—in the knowledge that she wanted him for everything he was and for eternity.

And knowing there was an eternity, their lovemaking was slow, delicious, perfect. They moved together without thought or question, reaching the summit as one.

The journey back was just as easy, just as satisfying. Michael pulled her closer into his arms. "Are you warm enough?"

"Mmm...toasty. Thanks for leaving my socks on." She snuggled against him. "How are you? Comfortable?"

Michael smiled—she looked adorable in nothing but her knee-highs. "This chair could use a little more padding, but it'll do."

"Good." She leaned back and squinted to see his face. "Because I'm not moving."

He reached around her and found her glasses, then slipped them on her. "Lost a contact?"

"Uh-uh." She took a deep breath. It was time to start being honest with him—about everything, always. "My eyes have been bothering me."

"Working too hard?"

"No. Crying too much."

"Aw, Katie..." He touched the tip of her nose with his, his eyes and voice filled with remorse. "I was such a fool. I'm sorry I hurt you."

"You'll hurt me again, Michael," she said softly. "It's a part of life—it happens. What matters is that we love each other and try to be kind."

He caught her lips in a slow, exquisite kiss. When he lifted his head, he said, "I can't believe I almost let you get away."

"I know." She squirmed on his lap, shifting so she could more fully face him. His response to her movement was instant and she smiled wickedly. "But you'll have to marry me to keep me."

Michael arched an eyebrow. "Is that a proposal?"

"Yes." She tilted her chin playfully. "I've learned it pays a girl to go after what she wants. Besides, my students are expecting a wedding and now that the blonde's out of the picture, there's no one else around for you to marry."

Michael lowered his head. "What would your students think about the day after tomorrow?"

"Oh, Michael...I don't know. There are the blood tests and my parents and—" As his lips caught hers, she forgot everything but the feel of his mouth on hers and the meaning behind the kiss. They had later to talk . . . and forever to be friends. Katherine sighed and pulled him closer.

*   *   *   *   *

SILHOUETTE Desire™

COMING NEXT MONTH

#541 SHIPS IN THE NIGHT—Dixie Browning
They were ships in the night, but no matter how much they
denied it—and deny it they did—Thaddeus Creed and
Gioia Murphy had found safe harbor in each other's arms.

#542 WINTER HEAT—Mary Lynn Baxter
Alison Young was wealthy and widowed and was expected to stay
that way. She wasn't supposed to take up with the likes of
renegade Rafe Beaumont—but there was no stopping her!

#543 TOO MANY BABIES—Raye Morgan
Freewheeling pilot Scott Bradley thought he was hallucinating
when he saw the tiny pajama-clad creatures in his apricot tree. He
didn't like kids, but their mother—*that* was a different story.

#544 CONVICTED OF LOVE—Lucy Gordon
Trying to help, lawyer Diana Waldman nearly blew undercover
policeman Lee Fortuno's cover. He had a job to do, but planned
to return to attend to their unfinished business!

#545 A PERFECT SEASON—Judith McWilliams
Christina wasn't about to play ball with ace pitcher Jace
McCormick. But then Jace threw her a couple of curves and
Christina couldn't wait for him to come home!

#546 FIRE AND RAIN—Elizabeth Lowell
Man of the Month, Luke MacKenzie swore his ranch was no
place for a woman—but Carla McQueen had the power to make
him eat his words.

AVAILABLE NOW:

SILHOUETTE Desire™

**Just when you thought all the good men
had gotten away along comes...**

MAN OF THE MONTH 1990

From January to December, you will once again have the chance
to go wild with Desire *and* with each *Man of the Month*—twelve
heart-stopping new heroes created by twelve of your favorite
authors.

Man of the Month 1990 kicks off with FIRE AND RAIN by
Elizabeth Lowell. And as the year continues, look for winning
love stories by Diana Palmer, Annette Broadrick, Ann Major and
many more.

You can be sure each and every *Man of the Month* is just as dy-
namic, masterful, intriguing, irritating and sexy as before. These
truly are men you'll want to get to know... and *love*.

So don't let these perfect heroes out of your sight. Get out there
and find your man!

MOM90-1

You'll flip . . . your pages won't!
Read paperbacks *hands-free* with

Book Mate • I

The perfect "mate" for all your romance paperbacks

Traveling • Vacationing • At Work • In Bed • Studying
• Cooking • Eating

Perfect size for all standard paperbacks, this wonderful invention makes reading a pure pleasure! Ingenious design holds paperback books OPEN and FLAT so even wind can't ruffle pages— leaves your hands free to do other things. Reinforced, wipe-clean vinyl-covered holder flexes to let you turn pages without undoing the strap . . . supports paperbacks so well, they have the strength of hardcovers!

Pages turn WITHOUT opening the strap.

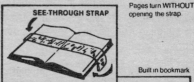

SEE-THROUGH STRAP

Reinforced back stays flat.

Built in bookmark

BOOK MARK

BACK COVER HOLDING STRIP

10" x 7¼", opened.
Snaps closed for easy carrying, too

Available now. Send your name, address, and zip code, along with a check or money order for just $5.95 + .75¢ for postage & handling (for a total of $6.70) payable to Reader Service to:

Reader Service
Bookmate Offer
901 Fuhrmann Blvd.
P.O. Box 1396
Buffalo, N.Y. 14269-1396

Offer not available in Canada
* New York and Iowa residents add appropriate sales tax.

BM-G